THE S~~H~~  ~~S~~

Beast
AND
the
Imp

STEPHANIE HUDSON

THE SHADOW IMP SERIES

To Jess,

BEAST
AND THE
IMP

Happy Reading

Beast and the Imp
The Shadow Imp Series #2
Copyright © 2021 Stephanie Hudson
Published by Hudson Indie Ink
www.hudsonindieink.com

Beast and the Imp/Stephanie Hudson – 1st ed.
ISBN-13 -

In true Pip fashion I decided to ask my kids what they would dedicate the books to. So here is my son Jack's dedication.

I dedicate this book to AquaMan

Thank you for keeping our oceans safe.

**As a side note, I personally thank you for being great eye candy and my husband thinks you're cool for drinking Guinness. **

STEPHANIE HUDSON

ONE

AN UNLIKELY FRIEND
LONDON
9TH OCTOBER 1680

I couldn't believe it.

I just couldn't believe it!

I mean, I'd heard the rumours, all of my kind had, for the King of Vampires was a legend. One that led many to believe he was untouchable, like some sort of myth. A nightmare told to demons to scare them. He was a ghost, a phantom, the most notorious killer and famous assassin for the King of Kings himself!

Oh, and not forgetting on top of all of this, he also

ruled over the entire vampire race… and now here he was, having just saved me.

Me.

"You're Lucius Septimus… as in, once emperor of Rome and assassin to the King… you're him!?" I said, clearly getting excited and also a little bit more terrified than before. At this, he expelled a groan of exasperation and said,

"Careful, darling, or you will be swaying for a different reason, and I believe the whole point of this is not to get fucked by me." Then he grabbed the rope that had been dangling around my neck and yanked it from me. After this, he pushed off the wall that he had been holding me against until my legs became steady, and put distance between us… something I thought was a good thing right now. Although, in truth, I think they were shaking more than before, now knowing who I was with.

Lucius Septimus… holy Hell and their Gods!

"So… erh… the King… he… he sent you to help me?" I asked in astonishment, and because of it, stuttering my words.

"Last I checked, little Imp, helping you also means helping contain a raging beast from destroying the world…

so yeah, the King sent me," was his arrogant answer. But then again, seeing who he was, then he had every right to be arrogant, especially since it was rumoured he was just as powerful as the King of Kings himself! This was because it was said that he had the power to control any mind, even that of the King. But then, if these rumours held merit, it made me wonder after seeing the bodies piled on the floor, why he hadn't just controlled their minds and made them simply walk away?

"Like I said, killing these four cretins was merely an unexpected reward, one that made what I imagined to be a dull night more interesting." I scoffed at this, now being brave to speak freely.

"Crickey, I wonder what other hobbies you have." My sarcastic tone was one he grinned at, before replying,

"I don't know, perhaps I am thinking of a new one right now."

"And what's that?" I asked, falling for it.

"It includes gagging and hogtying before seeing how long I can keep an Imp in my cellar." At least he winked at me, making me giggle, for clearly, he was speaking in jest… *at least I hoped he was.*

"Now come, the last I checked we are under some time

constraints here," he said, nodding for me to follow him.

"And where exactly are we going?" I asked, making him look me up and down and wrinkle his nose, before telling me,

"Somewhere I can get you clean of that stench first, for you smell like a Mongolian death worm." I rolled my eyes at this, and said,

"You do realise where I have been for the last eighty years, don't you?" At this, he granted me a look, and had there been more light I would have been able to read it, along with the rest of his features.

"It was mentioned, yes," he replied dryly.

"Mentioned, was it?" I replied with a roll of my eyes at the blasé way this was said.

"Like I said, you're not what I expected… not in person anyway," he replied cryptically.

"Do I want to know what that's supposed to mean?" I asked, folding my arms, a move that made me wince with a broken rib.

"Not in all likelihood, no… now if you please," he said, holding out his arm for me to proceed him down the alleyway and as we walked past the pile of bodies, he clicked his fingers and they all ignited into a blazing flame.

"Is setting things alight another hobby of yours?" I asked in jest, making him smirk.

"I have rope in the carriage, little one, don't tempt me to use it." I chuckled at this, as I understood this was clearly how it was going to be between us. This camaraderie was one that I had to admit was refreshing, as I didn't expect someone as notorious as Lucius Septimus to even have a sense of humour, let alone to not have strangled me yet. Then again, he was here to help me, so that would have made helping me a bit of a moot point should I be dead.

"Sounds exciting," I answered back, making him shake his head a little as if he didn't know what to do with me. Something that tended to happen quite a lot around me.

"They said you were going to be trouble," he commented, with one side of his lips lifting as if he were enjoying himself.

"But isn't that the best kind of fun?" I challenged.

"They also said that you and I would get along swimmingly," he told me, making me laugh once before asking,

"And do you like swimming?" At this, he smirked once before answering,

"Fuck no."

His reply made me really laugh this time as he led me to what I could now see was a carriage waiting for him. I wanted to ask where we were going but in truth, I didn't really care. All I knew was that hopefully it was somewhere I could get clean before crawling into a bed and sleeping through the process of my body healing.

Lucius held a what was still bloody hand out to me like a gentleman, to help me into the carriage. Soon after this, he was closing the door and we were on our way to an unknown destination I hoped possessed a bed. But then, as soon as we started to travel through the city, I was amazed to see large lanterns aflame inside glass cages, providing a reprieve from the dark autumn night.

"Good lord," I uttered, making Lucius cock his head and say,

"That's me." I scoffed and said,

"Not you, the lights, they make the streets glow."

"Ah yes, it makes me miss Paris." I frowned in question, before he carried on explaining,

"There are many in Paris, they're far more proficient in lighting their streets than London can claim, but it is a start, I suppose," he said with a shrug of his large shoulders. Something I could see now that more light awarded me his features. Gods, but he was handsome, quite possibly the most handsome man I had ever seen, even if I was only being granted mere glimpses of such raw beauty as we travelled.

He had strong features, with piercing eyes the colour of a winter lake, not quite blue and not quite grey, but a startling place in between that when cast your way, you didn't just see them, but you felt the gaze, one that locked you there until he was finished with you. Like many before him, he wore a long black wig of curls, as was the fashion and well, as supernaturals we weren't in the business of standing out, but instead... blending in. Yet, despite this, I had a feeling that his natural hair that was hidden was of a much lighter colour. If his brows were anything to go by, I would have said the colour of desert sand. As for his lips, they were perfect in their shape and made even more lovely and enticing when he graced you with a smile, one I grant you, I had only seen in the dark but it had been enough to make the claim.

It made me look forward to the morrow, as I knew I would see him fully in the light of day... although as a Vampire, I knew they disliked the daylight but was their King the same? I had heard somewhere that it was fated to change, just like many things that were rumoured to happen. This, along with a shift of power the Kings would all experience once the prophecy started with the King of Kings finding his own Chosen One. But then, as an Imp of little importance, this was all just speculation on my part, for I could not claim to know much beyond my own fate at present.

"It would no doubt be prudent to mention that I've found him," I told Lucius, after he watched me for a street or two as I looked in wonder at the lights we passed.

"So soon?" he asked in return.

"So, you know who I'm talking about?"

"Let it be understood that I have been well informed on this assignment, little Imp. So yes, I know who you are referring to."

"Gods," I uttered, shaking my head and wondering if at any moment it wouldn't just keep spinning, for I was overwhelmed.

"The Gods are not the ones helping you now, you can be assured of that," he said, taking my meaning for another.

"Oh, trust me, I know that, and enough to remember quite well without being reminded of such," I said, making him raise a brow in question before putting it into words.

"Then what did I speak of that prompted such a reaction?"

"Well… it's just that it seems as if everyone knows about me," I admitted after a sigh.

"And what of it?"

"I can declare with honesty it being a first, that is the truth of it," I replied.

"I have known many a Being before their name was well known to others, yet fate turned the tides on their lives all the same," he told me, making me frown before pushing for more.

"And?"

"It means that the river doesn't just stop flowing because you ask of it to do so, little Imp… just as the Fates do not stop leading the unknown down the paths they are destined to travel."

"The unknown… that was me. For before I got sentenced to Hell, no one knew my name. No one knew anything about me. I was just another lowly Imp wandering the world, and now I'm visited by royalty on the hour." At this, Lucius laughed and said,

"Things change for us all, little darling, for one day you are nothing and the next your entire world has been changed and suddenly you are something far greater than you ever thought possible."

"I gather you're speaking from experience?" I asked, as he certainly seemed to understand the way of things.

"Simply put… there is only one of us in this carriage that was once born human and it isn't you, little conker." I sucked in a quick breath, not knowing what surprised me more, the fact that he had once been human or that he knew exactly what Imps were born from. Because in truth, it wasn't exactly common knowledge, even for a demon close to our realm.

But then again… Lucius wasn't just any demon.

He was the King of an entire race of them.

After this, we resumed our journey in silence and, thanks to the dark streets and the rocking motion of the carriage, I soon fell asleep. In fact, the only time I stirred was when I felt myself being lifted and held in a strong pair of arms. A short time later I felt the soft dip of a bed, then nothing else.

Emotional exhaustion took over.

However, an unknown amount of time later I started to tug at the edges of sleep the moment when I heard voices in the room.

"Will she be alright, I heard about the attack?" I recognised the voice as belonging to Sophia Draven, the King's sister. Honestly, had I the energy, I would have opened my eyes and hugged who I now considered the only friend I had in the mortal realm, because this was what she had told me before I was sentenced. That we were one day to become friends, making me wonder if that day was soon.

"Fear not, as I made them suffer," Lucius' stern voice said, doing so in such a way that he seemed far angrier about the memory of it, than during the act itself. Unless he had wanted to contain his rage on my behalf?

"Good, my only regret is that I wasn't there with you to add to their suffering," Sophia replied, making me want to smile.

"She suffered some injuries, but her body should be healing... I have to say that I was somewhat surprised that it hadn't started to heal instantly, as I think an important aspect was left out when this assignment was being described to me." After this, I heard Sophia Draven release a heavy sigh before telling Lucius what I thought no one knew.

"It is true, she has no powers beyond a few supernatural

abilities, and it is why Lucifer refers to her as a youngling, for it is as though she has never been shown anything by her mentor, as if she was merely shunned for some reason before any training could ensue." At this, I bit down on my pillow, grateful that my face was away from them, and they could not see me or my reaction to their conversation. I also continued to keep my eyes closed, trying to convince myself in vain that this was still a dream. I felt so embarrassed by the truth because it had felt as if I had been abandoned. As though everyone had given up on me because I had been different, and no one knew how to handle something different.

But then the next words spoken quite honestly shook me to my core,

"She is certainly special," Lucius said, and suddenly my heart soared because I had never ever heard another living being ever consider me as such.

"I told you she was, which is why she needs our protection, Luc," Sophia agreed and again, I felt the sentiment fire straight to my heart.

"She will have it, I give you my word," Lucius vowed, in a tone that no one would have dared challenge to be insincere.

"Be good to her, Luc, the Gods know she has not had it easy."

"That is true, but in my experience, what the Gods do not make easy for you, you simply learn the hardest lessons for yourself and with it, you become stronger," Lucius replied, and I had to say that he was shaping up to being an incredibly wise vampire... albeit a dangerous one.

"Well, she is under your wings now, so teach her well. Oh, and the reason I am here... give her these," Sophia said, and Lucius' reply quickly granted me knowledge as to what she was referring to.

"Why would she need these, I was led to believe she gave them back to you to pass back to the Oracle?"

"That's the curious thing," Sophia replied making me the curious one.

"I tried to give them back to the Oracle," she told him, and I could have just imagined in that moment him frowning.

"And, what of the exchange?"

"She said that her fated journey did not begin in Hell, it began the moment she did the right thing by stealing back those stones." Once more, Sophia surprised me and made it ever more difficult not to react. As for my mental state, well I still wasn't convinced this wasn't just all a dream.

"And what was that supposed to mean for her future?"

"The Oracle said that the stones have chosen, for she will be the first to be granted the power to use them, before they are then gifted to another." Her reply to his question continued to shock and from the sounds of it, I wasn't the only one.

"And when exactly is she fated to use a weapon such as these?"

"She knew you would ask this and told me to tell you to look to the skies on the 14th of November, for the great comet will travel over and align the stones making it possible for the first moon's phase to combine the Beast with her mortal." It was after she said this that I knew for certain this was no dream I was caught in. No, for this must be true. Because like most who knew of this plan, each of us were wondering how such a being could be contained within a mere mortal vessel and survive such a thing… well, now I knew and so did Lucius.

"Well, I believe we will need all the fortune we can get, so I will take what I can get for if this does not work, we all know the outcome of such an event."

"Trust in the Fates, Lucius, after all…" Sophia paused,

and I heard the patting of a hand no doubt against his chest as she said,

"There is even a fated one out there somewhere made for you... or at least..."

"There soon might be."

STEPHANIE HUDSON

TWO

ONE MOMENT
PRESENT DAY

After Amelia had finished at least some of her lunch, I asked if she wanted to play a game with me on the rug by the windows. This was at the other end of the room from where the grownups were still eating. As for me, I hadn't been able to take so much as a bite. This was because the longer I sat there woefully wondering when my snuggle bubble would show, the more my stomach tied itself in knots. This was to the point where I was starting feel sick and knew I needed a distraction. Well, for a big kid like me, there was no greater distraction than a child…

one who now had no vegetables left on her plate.

Although, it had to be said that she had managed only to eat one piece of carrot and two pieces of broccoli. Something that went unnoticed, mainly thanks to Vincent who made the rest disappear. But then again, he wasn't the only one fighting her vegetable cause, as her own father managed to sneak a few off her plate... only when his wife wasn't looking, of course.

In fact, it was usually at this point that she moved over to her father's lap and started stealing the food she did like from his plate... like when dessert was served. She always knew to sit on Daddy's lap for that.

After all, she was a clever cookie monster.

So, as the rest finished their meals, I finished the part when Lucius saved me, telling her the next chapter as we played Ker-Plunk on the floor, although I had secretly filled the tube with candy balls instead of marbles to make it more fun.

"Oh wow... he was like your hero," Little Bean said in a dreamy voice, now holding her little hands together by her chest. Of course, like all of the chapters I had told her so far, I had kept out the none-toddler friendly parts, meaning that Lucius had just saved me from a bad man who tried to steal my purse. One that called me nasty names, like smelly belly nelly, and being mean with words, not his fists. And trust me, to a three year old who was already a hopeless romantic, this was 'swoon over the hero' worthy.

"He was, but I wanted a different hero and, in the end, I finally got him," I told her with a wink before popping my sweet winnings into my mouth.

"You mean Uncle Adam saved you too?" she asked with her big blue eyes going wider.

"He did, and that time was even better than when the Vampire King did it." At this, she sat back against the wall and said on a breathy sigh,

"Wow. I wish a vampire king would save me." I laughed at this, knowing there was a high probability of it happening in the future... that was if the Fates had anything to do with it.

After this, Little Bean and I continued to spend the day together. This was after Keira followed us both into the sitting room, and after Amelia ran over to the fort that was still there from this morning. Then, with her daughter busy talking to her dolls, Toots took me to one side and asked me,

"I'm really sorry to do this but would you mind

watching her for the rest of the day, it's just that there's the meeting of the Kings tonight, and Lucius has just arrived and…"

"Is he talking to Adam?" I asked quickly, knowing how close they were. In fact, not many people knew this, but Adam and Lucius were BFF's! Not like a bromance type of deal but they were tight. But like I said, this was kept on the low down as they both decided it was best to keep things hush hush. This was ever since Lucius' involvement back in 1680, as he hadn't just saved my life that night, he also became the rock I needed to survive everything after that point. He had been there for me, and in more ways than just a simple order from his king.

Making this long ass statement shorter… we became friends. Actually, it was more like family. Because he didn't just help me find Adam and then send me on my merry way with my new boyfriend, he supported us both and helped us understand our powers. He became not just a mentor to me but to Adam also. And it was through this guidance that a strong bond formed between Adam and his maker. Which meant Amelia had said it best…

Lucius had been my hero.

So, seeing as the three of us were very close, as history

had made it that way, I knew if there was one person Adam would speak to, it would be Lucius.

"I'm sorry, honey, I don't know. As usual, Lucius is being weird, and since he stopped coming to events, it means he is only ever here when he has to be, like tonight for this meeting," Toots said with a frown, as it was true. Since Amelia had been born, Lucius had made every excuse possible to stay away until the point where he just stopped making them all together.

"Then, if you don't know where he is now, I can guarantee he's talking to Adam," I said before I started chewing nervously on my nail, one that was currently cut short so I wouldn't accidently catch Little Bean and scratch her. They were usually long and pointed as Adam liked a little scratching in the bedroom... especially when I combined it with outfits like my naughty kitten, complete with the furry tail butt plug I got for my birthday once.

"Then that's a good thing, right?" Toots asked, making me shrug and say,

"I guess so."

"Don't worry, it will be a bit of man talk and he will be back... plus, you know if anyone will be on your side, it's Lucius, you're like a little sister to him." I released a sigh and nodded, but it was unconvincing, so she nudged my shoulder and said,

"Trust me, you will see, Luc will tell him to get his head out of his ass and say something like... I am the man, Adam, the Vampire boss man and you must do as I say... now go back there and punish your wife the way she loves," she said, putting on a ridiculously deep voice when mocking Luc, making me burst out laughing.

"Alright, now that's settled, stop worrying and go do what you do best."

"Which is?"

"Well, a number of things, but right now it's being an awesome Aunt." At this I grinned and said,

"Fudge yeah!"

"I will try and get back in time to tuck her in and tell her a bedtime story, but it's going to be tight."

"It's okay, I'll bring her to you so you can say goodnight before the meeting starts. You know I love spending time with her and anyway, it's not like I have anyone else to spend time with at the moment... say, my own husband for example," I groaned, making her give me a sad look.

"Aww come on, you know Adam, I think this last test was just a bit too much. Remember, it's not only him whose limits are being tested… as I think this is proving the point that you also have to learn your own limits, Pip." Now this sigh was the biggest yet and felt as if I was deflating.

"I know you're right… seriously, when was it that you got so smart… no wait, don't tell me, I remember now… it was when some crazy cool chick kidnapped your beanie hind, and you woke up on a plane with me talking about cartoons." She laughed at this, considering this was exactly how we met.

"Well, it was definitely enlightening," Toots agreed.

"But of course, just call me the Dalai Cartoon Lama. So, big meeting, eh?" This was when her face got serious and she moved closer to me to say,

"Yeah, it's terrible…"

"What's terrible?" She then took a deep breath and told me…

"Some girl has gone missing."

THREE

RIP BARRY AND STEVIE

As soon as she whispered this, doing so to make sure Amelia wouldn't hear, I frowned.

"Erh, not to sound harsh here or anything, but girls go missing all the time and we don't get involved. That's not to say we shouldn't. Hey, you know what, we could totally like set up a supernatural Scooby-Doo gang. Plus, I've always wanted a Great Dane, oh and bagsy Thelma."

"Really?" Toots asked, with one of those 'are you for real?' looks.

"Well, you're clearly Daphne, hello blondie," I pointed out.

"And Sophia, who's she gonna be, *Fred?*"

"Well, she's not going to be Shaggy, jeez she'd kill me." Toots laughed at this and said,

"Anyway, getting away from the supernatural Scooby-Doo gang, and no, before you say anything, you're not going to rush out and buy a mystery machine... this girl was taken by some supernatural guy, that's why we are getting involved."

"Seriously, Toots, come on!"

"What?"

"Supernatural guy... really? You've been a part of this family now for like a small forever, you're going to have to start learning the terminology and correct linguino soon."

"Says you, I mean you make most of the... *shit*... up!" Toots whispered the word shit, because, well... Little Bean was within earshot.

"I do not," I stated, before she folded her arms, cocked out a hip and said,

"Really, linguino?" I huffed keeping back from smiling as we continued our game.

"Say, didn't you used to work in a library and enjoy reading books?" I said, calling her out, to which she rolled her eyes.

"Are you kidding me, do you know how many demons and angels and creatures and mythology and Gods and realms there are? And plus, half the books in Afterlife's library are in different languages and I barely remember any Spanish as it is. Besides, I used to collect stickers when I was a kid."

"And?" I asked, wondering what that cool hobby had to do with anything.

"And I wasn't exactly collecting baseball style cards with demons on and their statistics."

"You know that's called Top Trumps, right?" She rolled her eyes again and said,

"Thank you, Pip, you are, as always, a never-ending source of random information." I giggled at this as I knew she wasn't being serious, plus she was currently trying not to laugh.

"Yep, just call me your friendly neighbourhood Imp, that may or may not, but most likely does have, a Spiderman onesie."

"I already know you do because I bought it for you for Christmas, and Adam bought you the web shooters to match." Now that was a great Christmas and turned out to be even better in the bedroom after I attacked him, sexually pretending he was the villain and needed to be fucked into a prison cell. Yep… great Christmas.

"Okay okay, fine, I'll wear it more often then."

"Okay, so not what I was getting at, but anyway, this case of the missing girl is a big deal for reasons we don't yet know, and I'm helping Draven compile what we do know," she said, making me wag my eyebrows at her, and say in a knowing dirty tone,

"Hell, yeah you are… compiling information… you dogs, you!"

"Seriously, how can you make that sound sexual?" she asked after shaking her head a little.

"I'm like Joey from Friends, it's a gift," I replied with a knowing and cocky shrug.

"Yes, well so is watching my child, so thank you, Pip… I just hate it when I have to spend the full day away from her," Keira said, looking at her daughter playing under all the tented material.

"I know, but she understands, plus she gets to hang out with her kick ass coolest aunt ever," I said, snapping my dungaree straps.

"Okay, but no dropping things off the roof this time, I really don't want the both of you firing water bombs and trying to hit the Kings' heads as they're walking into Afterlife… last time you got Jared's jacket wet and you know how he is about that bloody thing… geez, talk about paranoid, it survived a frigging Armageddon, so newsflash, it's going to survive water," Toots ranted, making me giggle.

"Okay, I promise, Tootie pinkies swear to a redonkulous goddess of awesome clothes. No playing on the roof," I said, making her grin at my unique but totally cool wording.

"Oh, and no candy from your room, we got you those 'we are closed' shutters for a reason," she said, making me put my hand on her arm and say in a serious tone,

"You don't have to worry anymore as I have some bad and upsetting news…" She frowned and asked,

"Why, what happened?"

"I am afraid that Oompa Loompa Barry, didn't make it."

"What do you mean Barry didn't make it, he's an animatronic, Pip, not a fish you won at the carnival." At this, I frowned as I held a finger up and said,

"Okay, now that totally wasn't my fault, Stevie was totally fine when I went to bed that night," I argued.

"Pip, you topped his bowl up with a bottle of vodka

you thought was water… Stevie died three sheets to the wind that night and pissed as a fart." Okay, so she had a point, I did do this.

"Okay, so yeah, it might have happened that way, but hey, at least Stevie died happy."

"And animatronic Barry, did he die happy too?" she asked as if she already knew the answer to this one.

"Let's just say he cannot make tea, and trying to force a boiling hot kettle in his hand didn't really work very well… but don't worry, Amelia was nowhere near… I'm crazy but I am not dangerous crazy," I said, making her sigh and tell me,

"You know you're a liability, right?" I grinned and said,

"I might know that, yes… but hey, it all worked out for the best as now he is a very attractive hat stand." At this she burst out laughing, which soon had me joining in, which was signalling the end to one of our usual weird conversations I adored. That was because Toots totally spoke Pip, whereas not many people did. Hence the Bestie beastie status.

"So, you still telling the story of Pip?" she asked, nodding to Amelia, who I was pretty sure was now acting out one of her male dolls as being a vampire and doing a roundhouse kick to the evil teddy that was trying to kidnap Disco Barbie. Although, I had to say, with the way she was spreading the male doll's legs whilst kicking, let's just say I doubt he was fathering kids anytime soon nor was he gonna get himself some after saving the girl… *ouch.*

"Yep, we just got to the part where Dom sent Lucius to save me." Keira narrowed her gaze a second as if deep in thought before saying,

"Wait a minute, when you told me how you met Adam…"

"Back in our awesome tea party tree, yep go on… got a mental picture now and it's great," I said interrupting her.

"Yes, it was fun, but when I asked you, you told me Draven didn't know you during this time?" Keira asked, obviously remembering this conversation like it was yesterday and now wondering why I'd lied back then. I opened my mouth ready to spill when in the end I didn't need to. Because it was at this point that the man himself walked in and answered her.

"Yes, because that's what I told her to say should she ever meet you." Keira frowned at her husband and asked,

"You knew she would?"

"Let's just say Sophia wasn't the only one privy to the Fates plans, as who do you think cast her sentence and why?" I released a sigh, now being the one to remember this as if it was yesterday.

"Yeah, and in your husband's defence, I should probably point out that he looked really bummed out about having to do it... like I could see your face King boss man, you so wanted me to stick around." At this, Dom's lips twitched as he found my reaction amusing.

"Seriously, it's like being married into a secret cult," Keira complained, making Dom pull her into his arms and tip up her chin so that she was looking up at him.

"Best not go back to cults, sweetheart, I am still touchy about the last one you were involved in."

"Yeah, well there is only one of us that is still having nightmares about itchy woollen shirts under hideous burlap dresses... besides, it wasn't exactly a holiday for me," Keira complained, making Dom pull her tighter into his huge muscular frame and say,

"Nor for me, sweetheart, *nor for me.*" At least she gave him soft eyes and cupped his cheek, then teasing him she tapped it twice and said,

"Get over it, handsome." Then she waved her ring

finger in front of him and said,

"We're married now, which means you can't get rid of me. Besides, I think history has taught you that you can't even hide in Hell without me finding you." At this, he threw his head back and burst out laughing as I swear this was Keira's superpower. She had the uncanny ability to be able to twist the past, no matter how upsetting, into something amusing and full of humour, so as not allowing you to focus on the past in a negative light but instead in a positive one. To be thankful you got through it and to beat back any bad memories with laughter. She was skilful like that. Of course, this wasn't to say she didn't pick her moments to do this, as she was also compassionate and understanding when the time called for it. But with her Draven, as she always called him, she refused to let his mind linger on the past. Besides, she loved making him laugh and had the ability to do so often.

"Are you ready?" the King asked her.

"Yeah, I was just asking Pip if she'd look after Amelia whilst I help you in the office." Dom nodded and then turned to me and said,

"Thank you, Pip, but please no more..."

"Water cannons off the roof... yeah yeah yeah, I got

it… I got it… consider me prewarned."

"And nothing with paint," he said, just to be sure.

"Look, wifey here already told me the roof is off limits." At this, I heard Amelia from inside the tent say a big,

"Awww, no fair," making me giggle, and just as I was about to open my mouth, Toots got in there first and said,

"No, no, Pip, don't say it." She was, of course, talking about my personal catchphrase, that I actually had on a variety of merchandise and had gifted to my extended family. The beach towel I was particularly fond of that said, 'ooops, I forgot to shave my fanny… my bad.' Naturally, the men weren't so fond of this one… although, thinking about it, neither were the girls.

"Look, don't worry, I got this and have looked after this kid a million times. We always have fun, and she's always wiped out and ready for bed, despite the number of sweets and candy she eats."

"Pip." This was said in a warning.

"Okay, okay, the shop is shut and will stay closed… plus the Oompa Loompa retired to become a snazzy hat wearer, remember…? I got this… Go, go." Toots gave me a hug and said,

"I'll see you later and don't worry about Adam, he'll be back before you know it." I gave her a nod and bit my bottom lip so that it wouldn't quiver. It just seemed as if the mention of Adam's name was enough to set me off, because there was a time long go where I would stand in front of the mirror after first hearing it and watch myself say it over and over again. Doing so like some lovesick fool desperate for just one moment with him.

And in the end,

One moment was all it took.

FOUR

HEROES KNOW BEST
LONDON
10TH OCTOBER 1680

Waking up this time finally felt as if I did so after some rest, and not just because it was a means of getting me from one place to another. I could already feel that I had healed from any injuries I had sustained from last night's debacle. I may not have had any real powers as such, but it had to be noted for small victories like last night when I had managed a little spark of power at least. But then, even with all of my concentration, all I had being able to manage had been what the likes of Lucius would no doubt class as a puff of wind.

This was the problem lay with my upbringing, or should I say lack of, as this was more befitting in describing my earlier life. Because all Imps at a young age need guidance, which was why when we became of age, we were usually appointed a mentor, someone to guide us in the right direction and teach us how to harness our powers.

But, being an outcast, I had never had this opportunity. As for the other supernatural elements of my being, there were of course certain things that came naturally. Things that happened without thought. Like my enhanced hearing, my heightened sense of both smell and sight. There was also added strength, more than you would usually find on an average mortal anyway. I was also quick in both my thinking and in speed. Something that thankfully aided me last night or all those thugs would have caught up with me, doing so a lot sooner... and before I managed to get to the theatre.

Before there was Adam.

I released a dreamy sigh as I focused once more on the memory of his voice. In fact, I knew I could have simply rolled over and probably fallen asleep for another twelve hours, but the memory of him was what made me pull back the covers and jump promptly out of bed. Then I tested my weight on my feet, rolling back and forth, happy and satisfied when I didn't feel any twinges of pain. That was when I knew for sure that the other natural element to my being an Imp had started to work.

My ability to heal.

Of course, what came next felt like another gift from the Gods, as at some point a copper bathtub had been filled and even though the water was no longer steaming hot, it wasn't freezing cold either. Had my dress not had some sentimental value to me, I would have ripped the thing to shreds just to get out of it quicker. But instead, I slipped it off and set it to one side gently as if it had been made from glass. I knew at some point I would clean it again and try and fix it the best way possible, even though I never wanted to wear the garment again. And, hopefully, I wouldn't need to as I didn't think showing up and allowing Adam to see me for the first time dressed as a beggar would help my situation.

I wanted to look pretty.

So pretty, in fact, that he instantly became beguiled by me and therefore hearing me speak would only solidify his admiration. That was, of course, if the first thing out of my mouth not be something foolish like declaring my love for him in an instant.

But as for the dress, well I kept it now for the sole reason that I wanted it as a reminder. Because I knew that every time I looked at that dress from this moment on, I would remember my time with Abaddon. Thinking back with nothing but fond memories and love in my heart.

So, I laid it gently on the back of a chair and stepped inside the tub, releasing a sigh the moment I did as it was pure bliss. As for the room that surrounded me, it was like the other I had woken up in, with rich furnishings and panelled wood that spoke of wealth and comfort. In fact, the only difference really was the colour scheme, for instead of lush shades of the peacock, this room was burgundy and gold.

"Well, I must say you're looking surprisingly better." The sound of Lucius' voice made me shriek, as I crossed my arms over my chest and shouted out,

"Ah!" Then I sat up quickly making the water splash over the sides, and upon opening my eyes I found Lucius now in the same room as me.

"What are you doing here!?" I asked in a tone that sounded accusing.

"Well, it is my house and come now, I never took Imps for being particularly modest," he said with a mischievous glint in his eye.

"Yes, well excuse me, but I have spent the last eighty years down in Hell with only one being ever seeing me naked."

"And your point?"

"That anything can turn a girl shy, even an Imp," I replied, making said point in an aggravated tone. However, he didn't take this seriously. No, instead he laughed as he walked past me, smirking down at me naked in the tub, before taking his seat off to one side. I wondered then what it was he had been laughing at, the fact that an Imp could be shy around him, or the idea of me and the Beast being together. Naturally, I didn't see the funny side to either one.

"Look, it is obvious you and I will be spending a great deal of time together from this point on, and considering we started off on a somewhat brutal front, I feel as though I should make myself completely understood," he said, picking something I couldn't see off his jacket, before tugging down the folded cuffs. This time, I could see more of him, thanks to the candles in the room. Ones now lit thanks to the fall of night, as it was clear I had slept the day away.

As for his state of dress, which currently was far more than my own, there was no colour to speak of, for his jacket was all black, including its buttons that lined either side of the opening. This was joined with a long waistcoat to match, one that finished before the knee and had slight accents of silver in its embroidery. As for his features, they were startlingly handsome as they had been last night. He was, at present, minus the usual curled wig, that still seemed to be so popular with men's fashion. This meant that I could see my earlier observation held merit, as his hair was the colour of desert sand, and long enough that it curled back from his face. This only managed to enhance the raw beauty that he held, along with an arrogant air about him that spoke of power.

"And how is that?" I asked now I had stopped observing him.

"I have no sexual attraction to you, nor will I ever feel inclined to take our unconventional friendship to any other level than what it stands at present," he told me in a blunt manner, and I didn't know whether to be relieved or insulted, hence why I said in jest,

"Crikey, you certainly know how to make a girl feel

special."

"I believe this should be of mutual agreement, considering we are here to find your Chosen One, a vessel for the one that you were fated to be with, therefore attraction shouldn't even come into it," he said, stating facts that were not only obvious, but were things I was already very well aware of.

"I agree, but that doesn't mean to say that a girl doesn't want to feel pretty," I replied, and at this he grinned. Then with a playful smirk lifting up his lips, he told me,

"I apologise, my Lady, please allow me to reiterate my past comment..." It was at this point that he bowed in an overly extravagant way, rolling an arm in front of him as if he'd been in front of a queen, making me giggle.

"My dear Lady, you are looking quite ravishing today now that the stench of London has been washed away from your skin." Again, this made me laugh and bow my head in return.

"Why I thank you, kind Sir," I replied with my own grin.

"Although, I do have to question if you were indeed in possession of soap during your time in Hell, as it looks as though you haven't washed your hair in decades... in fact, I'm not even sure what colour it is." I could tell at this point he was teasing me, but there was actually some truth to what he said. I knew this the moment he stood up from his chair and took possession of the soap that was in a box. One that contained all manner of beauty products. Then he handed it to me without once looking at my nakedness, thus proving the truth of his earlier claim. I could tell then that what he had said would never change, there was nothing sexual between us.

Of course, that wasn't to say that I didn't find him one of the most handsome men I'd ever seen. I would have had to have been blind not to. But then that was perhaps because I hadn't yet been graced with the good fortune to be granted sight of another, one whose very name made me swoon.

After this, Lucius reclaimed his seat as I continued to bathe, now having soap to aid me in this.

"We have many things to discuss, you and I, and very little time in which to pursue the reasons..." I interrupted and finished his statement,

"Your being here now." At this he inclined his head a little and repeated,

"Hence, my being here now." This was said in a

serious tone, as it was clear he took no pleasure by being here whilst I was naked, but like he said, time was of the essence. But this was when I started to wonder about what our time together would entail and because of such, it was why I suddenly blurted out my next question. One that clearly shocked him to his core…

"Are you married?"

FIVE

A CARING HAND

"*Are you married?*"
I asked, making him suddenly start coughing due to his shock before supplying me with his abrupt answer.

"Fuck no! Why do you ask such a thing?"

"I just wondered if there was a lady of the house, one I needed to be concerned of stabbing me in the back or trying to smother me in the night for taking the attention of her husband away from her." Now upon hear this, he grinned as if finding the idea highly amusing.

"There is no wife, nor will there ever be one, I can assure

you of that," he said with a certainty that surprised me, because it was not unusual for our own kind to find a soul mate of the same nature, and it was rumoured that all the kings were to one day find their Chosen Ones. Something, I confess, Lucius didn't seem all that enthusiastic about. Hence why I asked,

"Can you?" This made him raise a brow at me in question. I shrugged my shoulders as I continued to wash my legs, lifting them up out of the water and resting a foot on the rim.

"It's just that clearly the Fates have a way of surprising us all and if what they say is true, then there is a fated one for every king." This was something he scoffed at, as if the idea was a ridiculous notion.

"You don't wish to find your true love one day?" I asked, knowing full well that I sounded like a hopeless romantic. But then again this was hardly surprising considering the mere name of my own had me feeling lightheaded and giddy.

"Let me make myself perfectly clear, Imp, I don't make love... *ever.* And I doubt I ever will. But what I do enjoy is a good fuck... now don't take my meaning for anything but fact, for like I said, this isn't an invitation." I leant my head back against the rim and looked at him with a raise of my brow.

"I don't look at you like that, but I am not without my needs or my desires, which means that when I feel the urge to release some sexual frustrations, I act upon it like most of our kind do. That being said, I have no desire to take on a more permanent bed partner, nor am I likely to in the future… so, in short, you have no fear of backstabbing or being smothered in your sleep," he said, as if needing to defend himself and his cold reference to love.

"Well, if the Fates have taught me anything, it's to never say never." At this, he gave me another questioning look, so I offered him more of an explanation as to why I had come to this conclusion,

"Answer me this, Vampire… were you surprised when you heard the story of an Imp, one of little to no consequence, that had the power to tame Hell's greatest Beast and doing so, not with a spell cast or talent born, but instead by simply falling in love?"

"I think it was the most astounding story I'd ever heard," he answered honestly.

"Yet it happened," I stated.

"What is your point, Imp?" he said in a hard tone,

telling me that I was close to vexing him.

"My point is simple, you think the notion of eventually finding your true love, your Chosen One and the very being that will one day eventually become your wife, a ridiculous conception."

"I do," he added, making me go on.

"Yet surely it is not more ridiculous than the story you heard that day, one of an Imp who fell in love with a Hellish beast so powerful it could tear Hell apart, but more shocking still is that he fell in love with her in return... now knowing this, surely it would then be foolish to give weight to assumptions you yourself cannot be certain of," I said, knowing that I had made my point, when his stern features softened.

"Now, that is a point indeed," he admitted, and I granted him a little nod of my head before going back to washing myself, and saying in a boastful tone,

"And a well-made one at that, if I do say so myself." I then winked at him whilst grinning, making him roll his eyes in return.

"Well, there's one thing for certain," he commented.

"Yes, and pray tell, what is that?" I enquired.

"I have a feeling that from this day on, my life will most

certainly be more interesting and greatly more entertaining with you in it, of that last part I can be assured of." At this, I laughed and then bowed in the bath before telling him,

"Then I will take that as a compliment."

"And so you should, for it is the only one you're going to get until you do something with that hair of yours." I burst out laughing before I granted him a wink. Then I dunked my whole head under the water. A few seconds later I came back up for air, now with droplets running down my face and clinging to my lashes.

Then I turned to him and said in a playful manner,

"Better?" He took note of my teasing tone, and matched it with one of his own.

"Well, I can, at the very least, see that it's red, perhaps trying the soap might make me discover more." I chuckled at this and said,

"There's no treasure hidden there, if that's what you're wondering, nor is there any of your fine silver to be found... *for I have not had chance to steal that yet.*" At this, he threw his head back and laughed freely.

"So, getting back to our task at hand," he said, after I had rinsed my hair of the soap he had kindly provided me with.

"You mean, *Adam*," I said in a dreamy voice, and what his reaction to this was I would not know. I was too busy squeezing my hair free of the drops of water that remained, making it squeak as it was now that clean.

"Well, that is fortunate that *he* comes with a name. Shame then that there is quite a few Adams left in the world. Although, I grant you, even less so in London... let us hope then that he was not just passing through," Lucius commented, trying to weigh up our options of finding him.

"You think that's a possibility?" At this, he shrugged his shoulders and admitted,

"A slim one, perhaps... but one all the same. Which is why we need to act quickly."

"Well, I got his family name as well," I said, making him release a sigh of frustration and rub his forehead as if asking the Gods for patience. Then he muttered,

"Yes, that would be rather helpful... so?"

"So?" I questioned.

"This is the part where you tell me his name, my dear."

"Ah, oh but of course, Adam Fitzwilliam... that was his name." At this he tapped a fingertip on his lips, no doubt taking the time to ask himself if he had heard it before.

"Do you know him?" I asked, with the question almost

bursting from me.

"I don't recall, however, I have known quite a few Fitzwilliams in my time... this man you met, he was close to where I found you in Covent Garden?"

"Drury Lane actually, of course the last time I was there, there was no theatre to speak of," I commented, letting him know how much things had changed during my absence.

"Oh yes, a great many things have changed in the eighty years you were living out your sentence."

"Like?" I enquired, curious to know.

"The great fire of London for one."

"What?!" I cried out in shock.

"A large proportion of London burned down, I'm afraid to say."

"And the Cheese, did the Cheshire Cheese survive?" I asked in a desperate tone.

"I believe parts of the main structure survived, although it had to be rebuilt. Naturally, the cellars and underground caverns were untouched. Although, I could not claim the same for a lot of buildings, for most of London was decimated."

"And the cause of such devastation?" I asked, hoping it

was an accident and nothing more nefarious.

"It was believed to be one of our own, although naturally, this was not what the mortals have been led to believe," he told me, dashing that hope.

"Which was?"

"A bakery fire that got out of hand on Pudding Lane." I shrugged my shoulders and nodded my head, as this made sense and most certainly would have been plausible. It clearly must have been quite some sight if my own kind was unable to stop it.

"So that's why a lot of the buildings were new?" I mused to myself.

"Although, it has to be said, there was at least one positive outcome to arise from such desolation."

"And what was that?"

"Well, it managed to rid the streets of the plague." At this I tensed and gritted out through my teeth,

"That is kind of a sore subject with me."

"I can imagine it is," he said in a knowing tone, before nodding to me and asking,

"Are you finished?" I nodded, prompting him to grab a large piece of linen, one big enough to wrap around me, which is something I did after standing. Then he offered me his hand like he had done in the carriage. I found it endearing the way he was caring for me, yet it was as he had said before, I felt nothing but almost like a sisterly affection towards him. It was strange, almost as though I had always known him in this way. I also knew that in that moment, we were to become great friends, despite the obvious fact that we made for an unlikely pair.

"Thank you... you know you're not so bad for a king, in fact you're probably the best one I've met so far." At this his lips twitched, and he bowed his head in thanks. Then he held out his hand to a chair on the other side of the bed. This was to show me that there was a beautiful blue dress already laid out and waiting for me to put on. So, taking this as a hint, I dried myself and slipped on the garments, struggling with the back.

"Do you think you could help?" I finally asked, making him release a sigh and get from his chair to come and grant me aid once more.

"I confess I'm usually the one getting females out of their clothes, but I gather the process is the same, albeit in reverse," he commented, before coming up behind me and pulling at its ties so the dress would fit better.

"You are very little," he commented, before suddenly

spinning me around to face him and then pulling at the loose parts of the dress by my chest and belly. I looked down at myself and watched him do this before looking back up at him, as he was greatly taller than I.

"The ties are at their tightest so this will have to do for the time being."

"The time being?" I asked curiously.

"We will get you to a dressmaker soon, but until then, you'll have to do," he said in vague annoyance. However, I was shocked.

"You wish to buy me a new dress, one just for me?" On hearing this his eyes widened as if surprised by my question, before they softened as my reasoning became clear. Then he tapped me on the nose twice before telling me,

"From this moment on you are to be considered my ward, which means you will no longer find yourself scurrying along the slums of London, living in attics and wearing men's clothing, whilst drinking in the Cheese." I frowned in question, wondering how he knew all of that as it was much more than just a guess.

"You know all of that?"

"But of course, after all, who do you think it was who

found you after you skipped out on your trial." It was at this point, after making the obvious statement, I realised that he was right. After all, they had been hunting me, so it made sense Lucius had been appointed the job.

"Sure enough, you were easy to find, being a creature of habit that you are. After which, I informed the King, and the rest is history made by you," Lucius said, which wasn't surprising, seeing as it was said that he was the King's right hand man and well known as his best assassin. Which meant that he would have found me long before I would have ever seen him coming.

"I see it is now starting to take root… good, now come and sit down." I did as I was told after he took my hand and led me over to a long upholstered bench-style seat with sides and a back, that looked both comfortable for sitting and reclining. On his way to this seating area, he picked up a comb and just before I had chance to sit, he rolled a finger around over my head and said,

"Turn." I did as I was told and sat down with my back to him. This was when the oddest thing happened as he started to comb through my hair as if I was some doll of his to care for.

"There are more knots in here than a Se'irim demon,"

he complained, comparing me to a goat like demon that was known for its long-knotted hair that it often got all caught up in.

"I didn't exactly receive the care package when I went down into Hell eighty years ago," I snapped, making him chuckle before saying,

"No, I suppose not, for if they didn't even provide you with fucking soap, then I doubt they would have given you the means to comb your hair." Strangely, he said this in a hard tone as if the thought annoyed him. So as to ease this annoyance I shared with him what I did have.

"There was a natural spring that had minerals in it. This seemed to keep me clean at least, and as for the top pools, these were cooler and were for drinking."

"And you managed to care for yourself this way?" he enquired, as if he was genuinely curious to know.

"Well, mainly Abaddon was the one who took care of me." At this, the combing stopped as he was clearly shocked.

"How so, explain it to me for I wish to know."

"He would feed me, keep me warm and comforted. He would protect me and provide me with surprisingly good company. Everyone thinks of him as this weapon, this destructive force and one only made for killing. They think that is his only desire, but it is not true… he's simply misunderstood," I told him, getting annoyed on my Beast's behalf.

"And you went in there with an open heart, I guess, ready to be the one to understand him?" he asked, and I questioned if it was said to mock me.

"You don't believe it?" I snapped.

"Oh, sweetheart, I've known you for all of five minutes and here I am combing your hair, wondering when the last time you had food was, whilst also questioning how long it will take to get you dresses made," he said, shocking me to the point my body stilled. Then he released a sigh and explained further.

"It is, I grant you, a foreign feeling, but a feeling none the less and one some would call of a paternal nature. It is what it is, and I am not a man to ever feel ashamed of my actions. So, in answer to whether I believe or not, then you can trust me, for I can very well consider it to be the truth." At this, I grinned to myself and then told him in a gentle tone,

"Now, that was a good compliment." He chuckled once at this, and said,

"And not the first you will receive, no doubt, especially when we find this Adam of yours, for all we need to do now is find him and reunite you with your Beast... Gods help one Adam Fitzwilliam," he said, adding this on at the end and making me giggle. But then I thought back to what I had discovered last night, and knew now was the time to share what was most likely to be an important factor.

"Yes, about that, there might be a slight snag in the plan."

"Care to elaborate on what type of snag we are to encounter?" he asked, as he stopped combing a moment and he leaned close enough that I could see him in the corner of my eye. It was this point I released a deep sigh and told him what were possibly the most painful words I had said yet...

"I think he might be in love with another woman." At this he scoffed and commented,

"I don't foresee that being a problem for long."

"You don't? Why not? Are we going to kill her... wouldn't that be a bit wrong, not that I'm unwilling for that outcome to happen but I..." At this he burst out laughing, then he turned me by the shoulders so that I was now facing him again. He put down the comb and arranged my curls on either side of my face, giving me a soft smile.

Then he took hold of my chin and scanned my features, before telling me,

"With a face like this, trust me…" he paused to lean closer and whispered,

"He won't know what has hit him." I smiled, blushing at the compliment, but then something hit me with his words. This was as a plan started to form in my mind… and one so full of genius, I couldn't help but smack him on the top of his arm and shout,

"You've just given me a great idea on how to make him fall in love with me!" He rubbed the top of his arm and in a teasing manner said,

"Oww, by the way… and just what plan would this be?" This was when I gave him a mischievous look and told him,

"It's not the other woman I want you to kill…"

"It's me."

STEPHANIE HUDSON

SIX

THE HARLOT

"I just love it when a plan comes together," I said whilst currently spying on the theatre, waiting for Fitzwilliam to return.

"You know, I have a feeling that sentence will become a well-known saying one day," I added, making him cast a sideways glance my way.

"Don't get too hasty yet, I would hardly say that this plan has come together, for it is barely in its infancy," he commented dryly.

"Yes, but I get the distinct feeling that it's going to become a thing, like someone important is going to say it in the future and I just wanted you to know that… well, I said it first."

"Duly noted," he said dryly before adding,

"I have a feeling you will be the first at a great many things, little Imp." I grinned at him and admitted,

"I should probably let you know now that I am somewhat of a wordsmith and can claim quite a few that are still in use today or at least, I believe they are." At this he patted me on top of the head like a child, and then asked,

"Is perchance one of them, cramp-words?" I laughed, as this was a term used to describe difficult or obscure words.

"Ha ha very amusing, Mr Septimus," I replied, feigning my amusement, even though it was a witty remark that had been one I found amusing.

"I do try," was his wry response.

"Speaking of trying, what are we going to do about that?" I asked nodding ahead, as I now watched the woman I had seen last night enter the theatre dressed in her fancy clothes. It was discovered that she was a singer and was also the star of some play I couldn't pronounce, in a foreign language I didn't care to learn. A play that was currently having a term at the theatre. As for Lucius and me, after I told him my plan, which granted, at first he thought was absurd, he decided we needed to do some spying reconnaissance. This was to see what we were up against... or should I say... *who.*

Of course, when I first told him I wanted him to kill me, I didn't mean it in the literal sense. No, I just wanted him to make it look like a near death experience. He thought this notion was a ridiculous one until I asked him,

"Really and other than the taste of blood last night and a quick meal, did you not feel good about yourself when saving the damsel in distress?" He thought on this for a moment and then had to admit,

"You might be on to something, for I did get a great sense of satisfaction when the bastards died. But if you think the plan here is for me to pretend to attack you, only to then have him come in and save the day by me letting him punch me, then you are ..."

"No, that's not my plan," I interrupted quickly before he could claim I was insane.

"Thank fuck for that," he grumbled, making me grin.

"No, I think you are going to have to be in my life as some sort of family member, perhaps an uncle," I suggested, making him grant me a quick look of disbelief.

"How old do you think I look?" he asked haughtily.

"Not old, per se… but you look very… distinguished."
He grumbled again, rolled his wrist around and said,

"Better get to the plan before I become grey and start complaining about gout." I giggled, before saying,

"What I mean to say, is that Adam could save me from an accident befalling me. May be a runaway carriage, I'm sure that's still a thing."

"Carriage accidents are a common occurrence still, in fact it's actually not a bad idea." This was when I swatted the back of my hand to his chest and said,

"See, I do have them on occasion." His lips twitched again, and he gave me a knowing look.

"I believe you, little darling." I grinned at the endearment and felt myself in need to ask,

"Why do you call me darling?"

"Because, look at you, you look like a little doll. Now even more so when you no longer have that shit all over you," he said, making me scoff.

"You're not very flattering, are you?" At this, he grinned and said,

"No, I am not. But what I am, is honest." I shrugged my shoulders and said,

"Well, I have definitely been called worse things."

"Don't worry, I am sure in time I will come up with a few more pet names for you. But for now, it's darling or doll, so pick one."

"Or you could call me by my actual name." His look said it all, so I added,

"Darling is fine."

"Alright then, darling girl, let's go and find this man of yours."

And this concluded explaining my plan, which brought us to this moment back outside the theatre. One we were still watching the front of from his carriage.

"Do you really think he'll show up?" I asked, needing to fill the void of silence.

"Well, according to you he seemed besotted, and tonight is the last night she will be performing, so it stands to good reason that he will," Lucius replied without looking at me, keeping his focus on the entrance.

"I must confess, I am looking forward to finally discovering what he looks like," I said in a wistful tone, making him suddenly turn serious eyes my way before he said,

"Come again?"

"I'm looking forward to seeing what he looks like, I bet he's going to be handsome... do you think he'll be handsome?" I asked, but he didn't answer my question. No, instead what he did do was growl out a frustrated groan before rubbing his forehead with his palm. Once again, it was as if he was trying to ask the Gods for patience.

"What?" I enquired, finding his response to what I said odd... that was until he enlightened me.

"Darling, this genius plan of yours might have a very obvious flaw, and one that contributes greatly to the reasoning behind why we are now sat in my carriage waiting for a man to show up."

"And what's your point?" I asked, which was when he leaned in closer, as he was sat opposite me. Then, when close enough to take hold of my chin, he pointed out the obvious.

"You don't know what he looks like." It was in this moment that his words started to take hold, for he was right, we were currently sat waiting for a man to show up, one that could have come and gone a hundred times over and I wouldn't have known.

"Oh," I said, a sound that he then mimicked in a sterner tone,

"Yes... *oh.*"

"Perhaps we should just go in then," I suggested, making him respond with an exasperated tone saying,

"Yes, perhaps that is best."

So, this was precisely what we did, and this time going in there I didn't feel quite so unprepared as the first. It also had to be said that Lucius naturally expelled a certain authoritative air about him, as if no one would dare deny him or even question his being there. I didn't know whether this was because it was obvious he was of the elite society. Something clearly known given the way that he was expensively dressed. Or it could have been the fact that he was an imposing figure of a man. He was tall, far taller than most in fact, and he was also large of stature, being heavily built with muscles. A body and frame that looked serious enough to prove effective, should the moment arise. Which meant that, even to mortals, you could tell that Lucius was powerful. Hence, why most tended to give him a wide berth and as a result of this, they gave me one too.

"Pray tell, what is it this time that has you so amused?" he questioned, looking down at me side on.

"Just smiling," I said in a blasé tone, hoping he would

take my answer for what it was, a clear indication that I didn't want to answer him.

"Don't get me wrong, little Imp, the sight of a smile becomes you, but I am not foolish, darling."

"It's embarrassing," I admitted as I shrugged my shoulders, making him smirk down at me and then say in a seductive tone,

"Ah, but those are usually the best types of confessions."

"It's just that I've never felt like this before," I admitted, feeling myself blush.

"Like what?"

"I don't know... like, important. It's silly, but I'm not used to walking around next to someone who is respected or feared. If it was just me right now, I would be pushed along the streets, knocked into, and told to get out of the way. I would have been treated as though I were nothing but a nuisance to society. But with you I don't feel like that... like I said, I feel important," I said shrugging my shoulders again, as if it wasn't as important as it was to me. Which was why I was surprised by the look he gave me, as it wasn't one of arrogance or humour or even pity, but it was an affectionate one. His eyes turned soft, making small crinkles appear in the corners of them that gave him a more youthful appearance. Then, for no other reason than to comfort me and offer me solace, he told me,

"Right now, little darling, you are the most important being in the world, for it's one you will be saviour of… and all you have to do is be yourself." At this, he stepped behind me and took hold of my shoulders, before stretching out an arm in front of me towards the main entrance. Then he towered above me over my back, and said

"For in there is a man who will fall madly in love with you, and all for being your charming, beautiful self and nothing more. Now, let's go and discover what he looks like… yes?" After this I had tears in my eyes. Something he saw when he stepped in front of me, and he simply swiped them away from the apple of my cheek using the pad of his thumb. Then he tapped a bent finger under my chin before taking my hand and striding up the steps into the theatre with me.

It was by far the nicest thing anyone had ever said to me and no matter what, no matter how long I lived, whether it be another hundred years or another thousand, I would never forget those words.

I would never forget what they meant to me.

After experiencing this sweet moment together, we

navigated our way through the theatre until we came to the very place that I had seen Adam last night. And it was here, in the maze of hallways behind the stage, that I discovered the true nature of the vile and dishonest, for the foolish girl that Adam Fitzwilliam had decided to bestow his affections upon, was nothing more than a…

Harlot.

She played men with her beauty and prayed on hearts she believed were weak enough that they would be given away freely, and all because she enjoyed it when a man lavished her with not only attention but with jewels and other gifts. In fact, I believed prostitutes had more morals than she, for at the very least a man knew what he was getting, if only for the night.

But this woman clearly had been doing this a long time, for her expensive lifestyle was paid for by the heartbreak of others. For men who simply wanted sex had a place to go. They had a woman to pay, and needs were met in return. Both would then walk away with a little slice of what they wanted. It was a simple transaction.

But playing with someone's emotions *was not.* She had made Adam Fitzwilliam fall in her trap. As for her, coin could be earned over and over again, but for them, a broken heart was not so easily mended or compensated. There wasn't pain at the end of paying a whore for a night of pleasure. But there was, however, pain to be found when discovering that the woman you loved, only loved your coin and the depth of your purse.

She was cruel.

I knew that the moment we turned around a corner and there was a different man stood at her door, one that was lavishing her with attention. He too had gifts and, unlike with Adam, she paid for them by spreading her legs as she looked both ways down the hall before making her choice. When seeing no one of consequence, she took him by the lapel of his jacket and pulled him inside, giggling about how they would have to be quick for she was to be on stage soon.

"That bit…!" This cursed insult ended up finishing in the palm of Lucius' hand, as he covered my mouth and used it to prevent me from striding down the hallway as I was trying to do.

"She will get what's coming to her, little darling, but not yet. We need her to lead us to Adam, and he is all that matters." Lucius' words worked well enough to stop me. For he was right, because Adam was the only thing that mattered right now and unfortunately, that meant we needed her to be the bait. Then once we had finished with her, the next bait would become me, and I would be one to treat him far better… despite the dishonest encounter.

"Come on, we will watch the show in the hope of seeing your man." I nodded, thinking this was a good idea, and I told him,

"Alright, but I am not applauding for her when the songs are finished." At this he smiled and said,

"I have a better idea." He led me away just as I was about to enquire further and looked at me with a mysterious glint in his eyes. Then he told me,

"We will show our distinct displeasure whenever she sings, and whisper such among the aisles. After all… I can control the minds of others, and I have been in need of a reason to extend my practise in doing so." At this my eyes widened excitedly.

"Really?" I asked in a hopeful tone. Then he looked down at me, and with a grin he mused,

"I wonder just how many people in a theatre I can reach out to in one go… it should be fun finding out, don't you think?" He then winked at me and I, in turn, jumped up and down, clapping in glee before throwing my arms around him and giving him a kiss on the cheek.

Then I told him,

"I think that's the best idea I've ever heard, you're quite wonderful you know." This was when he smirked down at me before tucking my hand in the crook of his arm and saying,

"Yes, little Imp…"

"I know."

SEVEN

BOOBIES OR GIBLET'S?

"**R**eally?" Lucius asked in astonishment.

"What?" I asked with a frown.

"Seriously, *that's the guy?*" Lucius hissed in shock as we had now found Adam Fitzwilliam.

This, of course, had been once the show had ended, as it didn't take much to guess where we would find him at this point. So, with this thought in mind, we tried for a second time, slipping through the backstage entrance door, and heading towards her dressing room.

After all, I gathered this to be his last opportunity to let his feelings be known to the deceitful whore in a

Grecian dress. Of course, she wasn't going to be as happy as she usually was, thanks to Lucius making good on his word, for she barely got more than a handful of people to applaud her performance. Lucius had managed to let a few people slip through the net, so it wasn't completely obvious something was amiss. But in doing so, this meant that one of these people was Adam. Unfortunately, it also didn't award me much in the way of discovery. This was because the private box we sat in, thanks to Lucius being as rich as a sultan, meant that Adam remained out of sight having a box himself further along.

This also meant that I spent the entire performance staring at what I could see, which was merely a jacket covered arm and the hand that was attached.

But, despite his obvious attentions being directed her way, I did gain solace when she received hardly any applause. Grinning when I watched as her face crumbled into one of suffering and confusion, no doubt questioning her talents on this eve. Because of it, I felt the sweet victory as she received her dues, for I think a hit to her vanity had been her greatest weakness.

After this, I had nudged Lucius and granted him a look, telling him I was currently ridiculously happy, and the oddest thing in return... Lucius looked equally as happy that he had been able to give this to me.

Which brought us back to watching as Adam fumbled with yet another gift, keeping his back to us. The brown box was one he dropped at least twice before even being able to knock on the door. Again, I was just wishing that he would turn around and finally reveal himself to me, which was something he did just as I was replying to Lucius' expression of shock.

"Yes, that is what... *oh, Good Lord in a basket...*" I started to say the moment he finally turned to look our way, and unfortunately, I barely got a glimpse before I had to hide. But it had been enough. Enough, for in that single moment, I swear it was like fate had intervened and created a moment with perfection in mind. This was thanks to the orchestra that had started to play at the precise moment I saw him, as they must have been rehearsing something new for tomorrow's performance.

It had been some romantic melody and I swear I could almost see the sun shining on his face, as birds sang in the sky, and the wind caressed his beautiful hair back from his handsome face and...

"Err, hello... little Imp... come back to me now,"

Lucius said, clicking his fingers in front of my nose and bringing me out of my fictional world. But then, I didn't know if it was even possible, for I had now seen his face and I sighed as if I was living in a dream.

"Yes… that's the guy… *that's my Adam,*" I said in a wistful voice, and Lucius rolled his eyes and muttered sarcastically,

"Brilliant… the perfect candidate for saving the world and its realms from destruction and utter annihilation."

"Isn't he just… *oh my,*" I breathed out, now needing to fan myself as I felt my whole body responding and getting hot.

"Gods alive, it's like she's on opium… snap out of it, kid!" Lucius said, after giving me a little shake and trying to get me back to the land of the living. A place I actually wanted to be, especially now that I knew such perfection lived in the same world as I.

"Okay, focus and then stay focused, and then try and stay focused for a lot longer this time, because I keep losing you," Lucius said, and I knew he was right, I needed to get focused because we had a job to do… *a very important job.* The most important job in the world, which was getting that man into my bed… and saving the world, of course… but both were equally as important at this point in my mind.

"Alright, I'm back, what's the plan?" At this, Lucius looked down at me with a raised a brow and said,

"We already have a plan, remember…? Runaway carriage… save the damsel… feel like a hero and fall in love…any of this coming back to you now?" I grinned and smacked his arm before firing my finger at him and saying,

"It's back and firmly in here." I ended this by tapping the side of my head, making him raise a brow.

"Although, I did actually mean to ask what is the plan as in… right now and what are we going to do about… *that?*" I said, nodding to the hallway and to the sound of the Harlot making her excuses that could be heard from behind her door.

"Now we wait until he finishes making a fool out of himself and then follow him to see where he lives so we may discover everything we can about him… that's usually how it works," he commented, making me frown at the 'fool' part, but I thought it best right now to focus on the most important element we faced.

"Oh, alright, that sounds simple enough… apart from the bit where you want him to make a fool out of himself with a girl I want to maim, starting with her head before mounting it on a spike and recreating Vlad the Impaler's favourite pastime," I said, making him raise a surprised brow.

"Killing the Harlot will not help as it will only expose you as a cutthroat, demonic little Imp and right now, that is not what we are trying to achieve… the opposite in fact. So, instead of spilling blood in his name, let's try wooing him with your pretty doll face first… yes?" I grinned at this and added,

"And my charms."

"Yes, those too, and no doubt whatever other talents you may possess in the bedroom, for I have a feeling they won't be lacking," he commented dryly, making me wag my brows at him before winking.

"Oh, you're not wrong, for trust me, my talents are many… I mean, how many other Imps do you see claiming that they tamed a beast like Abaddon. You think I did all that with just luck and my charms, huh?" At this, Lucius pinched the top of his nose and closed his eyes as he grumbled,

"Please, I beg of you, refrain from painting a mental picture." I ignored this and told him,

"I showed him my boobies."

His eyes snapped open, and he said,

"I am almost afraid to ask, but alas, here it is… *boobies?"*

"Yeah, it's what I call my breasts… trust me, I really think that one will definitely catch on," I told him, looking down at my chest and moving my body as if I was trying to get them to dance.

"Gods," he muttered, shaking his head.

"No? Okay, so what about giblets?" At this he scoffed,

"Oh, that makes them sound very appealing."

"Really?"

"No, of course not!" he snapped, making me smirk.

"Alright, boobies it is then."

"Seriously… I have nothing," he said to himself, and I giggled before telling him,

"Well, I have a lot of somethings, but right now my fated one is now stood with the wrong woman… so if we can please get to the part where she ceases to exist for him, I would be much obliged."

"Then we are in agreement, and therefore in no need to continue discussing your…" he paused to look down at my chest and said,

"...Boobies." I grinned and nudged him as I whispered,

"Admit it, felt good didn't it... alright, alright, getting back to the important save the world stuff." I took a quick peak, to see Adam straightening his jacket as he had clearly knocked and was now waiting for her to open her door,

"Just a moment," the bitch end of a dog called again, and I instantly knew something was different about this night. I looked at Lucius, who seemed to be listening out for something. Then when he found it, he cast his cunning gaze to me before telling me...

"She is not alone."

EIGHT

FOOLISH HEARTS BREAK

"*What!?* " I hissed, although considering what we had discovered earlier, I didn't know why I was surprised. But, despite all reasoning, this still managed to make my blood boil. In truth, I was caught between the morals of right and wrong. I was thankful that she was of that type so that I felt no guilt when splitting these two apart, because she was clearly not a good person. So therefore I was spared of any shame or remorse I might have felt for intervening in their relationship. But as it stood, I would feel no such guilt on her behalf. However, it was Adam's feelings that I cared for, and I knew they were about to be crushed beneath her lies and deceit, and for that I hated her and utterly loathed her for being foolish enough to do that to him.

This was when I heard the door being opened and decided to take another look. I was granted with the handsome sight of Adam grinning after first straightening his dark navy jacket once more and making himself presentable. Something he would never have do with me because I would have taken him any way he came. He was utterly flawless in every way, the very epitome of perfection, one the Gods themselves could not equal and if I could have but just a mere touch…

"Focus, Imp," Lucius said, grasping my hand, one I hadn't realised had been reaching out towards him.

"I did it again, didn't I?"

"Yes, that you did, little Imp," was his exasperated reply.

"Look, we can't all be the epitome of cool," I commented, looking him up and down.

"Cool? I am not cold," he stated with a frown.

"I don't mean it like you're cold, it's just another word that I use to describe someone who is striking, confident, cocky, bordering along the egotistical… but I'm thinking that the word could also be used as other things… like, look at that cool hat, that type of thing," I said in hushed tones as we continued to watch the scene play out in front of us.

"I'm afraid I'm not following… the hat is cold?"

"No, the hat is coooool… as in great, as in the type of hat that you just had to have and when you wear… I've lost you again, haven't I?" I asked when his questioning frown didn't change.

"It is becoming a regular occurrence, this is true," he commented wryly.

"Trust me, it will catch on."

"Alright, darling… now I think you should go back to focusing on lusting over your intended, as it makes more sense than this word dribble that continues to come out of your mouth."

"It's not word dribble, it's word genius, you'll see… I will revolutionise the world just like Shakespeare did," I hissed.

"Well, until then, can we concentrate on saving it and get back to the task at hand, for I believe that is your man over there trying desperately to get into the undergarments of another woman." I cried out in whispered horror,

"What!" I hissed before turning my head and finding him reaching out to take her hand in his. This was when I could stand it no longer and I stepped out and began storming down the hallway before I was quickly grabbed from behind, picked up and forcefully turned to walk in the other direction. This was just as Adam and this Margaret, noticed me. Lucius, being in control, waved a hand in the air with his back to them and, masking his voice with a deeper tone, he said,

"Take no heed to us, just getting rid of an intruder… be about your business." Then, the moment we were once again concealed, he plonked me down and got in my face.

"I will only say this once, Winifred… *Stick. To. The. Plan.*"

"Yes, boss." Lucius released a heavy weighted sigh of frustration before turning back to the scene of what I hoped was not two lovers playing… *what's to be found up the harlot's skirts!*

"So, about this plan…" Lucius sighed again,

"Yes, little Imp?"

"Just remind me of this part of it."

"Leave this part of it to me, in fact, until you have to play the damsel in distress, leave everything up to that point to me," he said firmly, making me nod.

"Alright, that sounds good... I can do that." Lucius gave me a nod of his head in return, as if he was thankful we had this straightened out. But then, when I opened my mouth again to speak, he held a hand up and pointed a single finger an inch from my nose,

"Not another word." This was when I thought it wise to do what he said, even though I wanted to ask him exactly what leaving everything up to him entailed. However, it turned out that I didn't need to as after a moment more of concentration on Lucius' part, I heard another man speak from inside her dressing room.

"Are you going to tell that wet dick to fuck off yet, so that I can continue fucking you." At this, my mouth dropped open in utter shock for it was clear Lucius had made him say this, which was why I hit the side of his arm and hissed,

"That was a bit blunt and uncalled for, don't you think!?" At this, Lucius looked down at me with a smirk and said,

"Blunt is what he needed, trust me. I have a feeling this guy will be of the forgiving sort." I suppose what he said was true and perhaps that wasn't a bad thing considering

I tended to need a lot of forgiving. Yet, despite this, I still felt bad for him as I looked to see his face crumble as the truth of who he had fallen for was revealed.

"Who is that, Margaret?" he asked in a stern tone, and her face was a painting worth the paint, for it was classic, and I was at least thankful that she was getting what was coming to her. In all honesty, I would have been surprised if this had not happened a hundred times before. As men might have been easily led around by their cocks, but that didn't mean that they were foolish enough not to see the daylight in front of them. And the sun tended to have a habit of casting light on the truth of the day.

"Oh Fitzwilliam, did you really think that I would pick you over anyone else?" she asked in a mocking tone I wanted to kill her for.

"Excuse me!"

"Excuse me," we both said at the same time, only mine was whispered from where I stood and his was snapped at the girl. Lucius raised an eyebrow at me and muttered,

"Fuck me, but it must be the guy."

"I am not in love with you, Fitzwilliam, and nor will I ever be," the bitch said.

"So, what was your desired outcome to all of this, I

was just to continue to shower you with gifts, was that it… and to what end?" he asked and even I knew he was being naive. The woman laughed once and said,

"Until you realised that it takes a lot more than expensive gifts to win my heart and that of my hand." I huffed at this, and Lucius instinctively held me back, knowing that I was two shakes of a donkey's tail from beating her bloody.

"And what would it have taken exactly, spilling my blood on the floor, or cutting my heart out to give you the opportune moment to stamp on it physically?!" he shouted back, showing me a glimpse of an entirely different Adam. One that had a backbone and a stern tone I wanted used on me in the bedroom. He was magnificent! He was everything a man ought to be to a woman like me… I liked them strong in the bedroom. I hoped he had a firm hand that liked to punish my quivering flesh and a sexual nature that matched my own. I wanted him with such passion that the blazes of Hell would…

"And I've lost you again," Lucius said, bringing me back from my sexual thoughts. Suddenly the door was ripped open further from behind her and the man who appeared made me gasp as he shouted,

"Look, she wants you to fuck off, you Pansy ass!" I

realised then that it was the man who had chased me out of the theatre the first night I was here.

"She's fucking the stagehand… I swear, Shakespeare's behind writing this shit," I muttered to myself, before Lucius looked down at me as I had told him what had happened on my first encounter. At this Adam looked as if he was going to get into a brawl, as he raised himself up straighter, and moved Margaret to one side in a brisk motion. Then, without another word, he punched the man straight on and knocked him back to the floor with one hit. It was spectacular!

"Alright, I agree… he's definitely your man," Lucius said, as I had deflated back against the wall with a dreamy sigh, now fanning myself once more.

"Oh my… Adam."

"And there she goes again." I heard Lucius mutter, ignoring the startled gasp of Margaret,

"Fitzwilliam!"

"That name is dead to you, woman, I suggest you never use it again," Adam said, before turning on his heel and walking away.

"That's our cue, darling," Lucius said, now grabbing my hand and shaking me from yet another sexual illusion.

But then, as we passed the harlot, who was now leaning over the unconscious man and tapping his cheek to try and get him to come back, I stopped. Then with a disgusted tone, I told her,

"Shot through the heart, and you're to blame... you give love a bad name." Then I walked away, leaving her sobbing and as for me, I turned to Lucius and said,

"You know I think that would make great lyrics to a song... don't you think?" At this, he grinned to himself and shook his head a little, continuing to walk me through the theatre as we both followed the man of my dreams.

"So, what now?" I asked.

"Now we follow him to his home, and that way we can discover more about him before setting the next part of our plan into motion... come on, we don't want him to get into a carriage before we are outside," Lucius said, pulling me along with haste and making it so that I was nearly running next to him. This was, of course, what happened when little legs try to keep up with long legs that could outrun a cheetah.

But despite my short stature, we didn't lose him, as it became apparent at some point that he must have been overcome with heartache. Because he needed to stop to compose himself, I knew this as we found him leaning against a wall muttering to himself. He looked to be fighting with his own mind. In fact, when he looked as if he was going to turn around and storm back inside the theatre once again, Lucius intervened. I knew this when it was clear he was taking over the mind of a nearby mortal, and one who was within earshot of Adam.

"Aye, that Margaret sure be a fine romp... and one that's been known to give me the eye or two, if you know my meaning," a gentleman randomly said to his comrade as they walked past Adam. This made his eyes go wide, and his mouth drop open in shock as he quickly started to rethink his decision to go back into the theatre. This was after he grimaced with his features now twisting in anger before he pushed off the wall and stormed towards a line of carriages, one of which must have been his own. I knew that when he got in and barked an order at the rider, saying,

"Take me home and let's be done with this wretched place!"

I felt bad for him, yet I knew it was for his own good. A woman like that didn't deserve a man like him. Hell, I was even questioning whether a woman like me deserved him. But then the Fates had deemed it so, meaning there wasn't any real reason in questioning it. I vowed then that I would soon make him forget all about her, by simply making him happy, just as he deserved to be.

A little time later and in our own carriage we soon found ourselves outside of one of the grand homes near St. James' Park. We then watched as he strode up the steps with angry purpose before disappearing inside. I put my hand to the door ready to exit when Lucius stopped me.

"But I have to…" I tried to say when he shook his head.

"There will be time for that and trust me, now is not that time, little one." I released a deflated sigh and said in a small voice,

"But he is distraught."

"Yes, and he will do what most men do when afflicted with such."

"What's that?" I asked hoping it didn't include another woman, and one you paid for this time.

"It is simply this… he will drink himself into a state and no doubt cause ridicule to himself by being found by a servant the next day, passed out on the parlour floor. To which, said servant will advise he go walk off the effects of alcohol consumption by getting some fresh air," Lucius said, making my eyes widen.

"She will?" At this, Lucius smirked and then told me with a wink,

"Indeed."

This told me that Lucius knew this due to being the one to either manipulate her mind or that he intended to pass her enough coin to do so. Either way, I didn't ask which, for there was little point as it would not change the outcome. One I was desperate for.

"Tomorrow, then," I said on a sigh, looking out the window of the carriage and seeing a light emerge from one of the windows as a candle must have been lit.

"Tomorrow it is, so I advise we go back, and you get some rest."

"How can I ever sleep, Lucius?"

"Well sleep you must, for after all…"

"Tomorrow is the first day of the rest of your life."

NINE

PUNISHMENT
ADAM
PRESENT DAY

"*Gods, Winifred!*" I hissed as I turned my back on a sight I loathed to see. I hated upsetting her, knowing that this was one punishment she would not enjoy. It pained me to say, but this time my Winnie had gone too far. What she didn't know was that after I woke up and discovered that damn ransom note, I had come the closest to a full shift than I had in a long time, which meant the dangers I could have put this entire household in were unthinkable!

Of course, after spending hundreds of years with my delectable little wife, I had learned patience 100,000 times over. This didn't bother me, as most of the time I found it amusing and endearing. I loved watching her exuberance for life. She had so many sides to her that even after all of this time together, I still found myself surprised on a daily basis, for that was my Pipper, my Winnie, she was never boring and hardly ever predictable.

She was the very meaning of being free spirited and I learned quite quickly that she held none of herself back like most people did. There were no games of emotion played on her part, only games of a mischievous nature. This was mainly due, in part, to my own fault. As her sexual appetite most definitely leaned closer towards the rougher side of sex. She adored being punished, playing 'the brat' often enough to get her way and she was addicted to my firm hand. Therefore, it was games of a sexual nature that we played, and the rules were simple. We never took it too far, as to inflict pain on our hearts and play with each other's emotions...

Until this day.

This day when she had played with mine.

I knew this, the moment I finally was able to get a hold

of myself and was strong enough to push back the beast of Abaddon, convincing him of her mistake. Abaddon was my counterpart in this life, and one I shared both my vessel and my soul with. Which meant we were both in agreement that we would need to teach our Winnie a lesson that she had gone too far this time, and for my wife, that meant a different sort of punishment and one that didn't include our conventional punishment at all.

Because to be honest, Pip's only weakness *was me*.

Although, she was not alone in this, as it was obvious to anyone that had eyes, that she was my only weakness in return. Which meant I knew the only way to get through to her and for it to be a lesson learned, was to deny her myself.

So, I spent the day torturing us both.

But this wasn't to say that I didn't keep my eye on her. And nor did I need to point out that every time I did it was like an arrow to the heart. I would hear her asking Keira if she had seen me and if she knew where I was. The longing in her voice made me clench my fists by my sides as I hid behind the door. I was forced to close my eyes, willing myself to stay still so as not to give in. This time I needed more than a simple hour away from her. This time the punishment had to at least last all day, or she would learn nothing.

In a way, she had always been like a whimsical child, for she was often as naive as she was mischievous. She was every single end of every spectrum, being the funniest person around to the silliest, and yet her wit and intelligence often took my breath away. There didn't seem to be a problem she could not solve, and despite this child like innocence she maintained, I was blessed to say that she was all woman! Her sexual appetite was a constant diversion, as it was hard to ever want to leave the bedroom. In fact, her favourite game to play was creating new ways to sexually distract me and the woman had more sexy outfits then I even thought possible! Every fucking fantasy you could think of and there she would be, walking out dressed like sin itself and I would be lost to the sight of her.

In all honestly, I was somewhat ashamed to admit that I could barely keep up with her, as it was the only time I really saw the demon in her coming out. She did not like to be denied and watching her sulk because of it, had caused many moments of amusement. I lived to tease her, for her reactions were like a gift. However, unlike her in this department, I knew never to go too far as I was well aware of her limits.

I just wished that she would be more considerate of my own.

But she was also my addiction, which meant that what I did now I did not relish in… *not one little bit.*

Every time throughout the day I had spied on her, I only ended up making it harder on myself. Because as the day drew on, my only wish was to go in there and scoop her up into my arms and take her back to our secret space. Once there, I would not chain her up or fuck her into an oblivion. I would not lay her across my lap and spank her like a naughty schoolgirl until her ass was glowing. Nor would I tie her to the bed and force her to come until tears formed from her eyes and she was begging me to stop.

No, this time I would simply lay her down and make love to my wife and in doing so, pour my heart out to her without the need for words. That was how I intended to end the day.

This fucked up awful day!

In fact, the only pleasure I received from it so far was the pleasure gained from watching her as she played with who was affectionately known as Little Bean. Amelia undoubtedly had a best friend in Pip, and the pleasure my wife got from spending time with her was both a beautiful and bitter sight.

Bitter because I knew how wonderful a mother she would have made and to this day it had been the one thing that I had never been able to give her. This, of course, was not through lack of trying for like she often said, we would put bunnies to shame with our fucking.

I would have loved nothing more than to have been able to create a little slice of ourselves in giving her a child. But Imps didn't give birth, they were merely born from something called the Mother Tree. Surprisingly enough, this information I hadn't learned from Pip, for it was the only thing she had not exactly been forthcoming about. However, what Winifred didn't understand was that as soon as I was connected to the Beast, his constant presence wasn't the only thing granted to me… I was also gifted with eighty years' worth of his memories to combine with my own. She was our beautiful wife, and one we both laid claim to.

A woman we both loved and would happily die for.

Which was why I also spent the day arguing with my beast as he too found it harder to bear as the hours passed. Which meant I had to be the strong one for the two of us, now trying to explain to him in my mind how this was for her own good. How I was not being cruel just for the sake of it. In fact, the only way I got him to back down and from breaking free once more, was to prove his own point was by arguing a better one of my own.

The tale of the boy and the wolf.

It had been like telling a child a story and if anyone had come across me, they would have found me on the rooftop talking to myself and telling myself this story. The premise, of course, was that a believed lie told so many times will only ever be a lie, even when it is a truth. But by that point the damage is already done and should she, Gods forbid it, ever really be kidnapped, then I needed to believe that it was true and not convince myself it was simply another lie.

Of course, I knew why she continued to push me in this way. I was no fool, as I had in fact learned this lesson the hard way. It had been not long after first joining with Abaddon and the first lesson had been about control. One taught on a day I would never forget, for it was one that could have potentially had grave consequences for both myself and my demon... *we could have lost our Winnie.*

So, at the depth of it, I did not blame her, but I had come to question her methods many a time before now, for they were not simply getting more radical, they were getting outright dangerous. Something I could not allow to happen again.

Because being away from Winifred was painful in more ways than anyone could imagine as I was not only fighting my own urges and my own addiction, but also that of one of the most powerful beasts in all of Hell's creation. On the most part it hadn't taken long for us to have been combined for him to respect my decisions.

However, with Winnie being his only weakness, it also meant fighting not only my own instincts but also his. Of course, our centuries shared together had not been without its hiccups, for we were married after all. Which meant I very much doubted a single couple in the world that could claim marital bliss without its disputes or ups and downs.

But, despite this, Winnie was my everything. She was my heart in its entirety, and the reason it beat was to keep my vessel living so I may stand by her side. The moment I learned that this was all fated, in all honesty, I didn't really care. I didn't care whether it was a destiny dictated by the Gods. No one could make me feel this way. No one could make me feel this strongly or be this affected by a woman, Fates be damned. And ever since that first day of seeing her, not one single moment passed me by where I was not thankful for every moment that had led both of us to the point of meeting.

A day I would never forget, not as long as I had breath in me.

However, that was not to say that it was without its difficulties for I was most certainly not the same man I was on the 11th of October 1680, a date I would never forget.

The date my heart was given to another.

To my Winnie, for she had my heart that day and...

Every day since.

TEN

BITTERNESS AND ENVY
LONDON
11TH OCTOBER 1680

"Sir… I'd be begging your pardon, Sir."

I released a groan and even that hurt, for it seemed as if the pain I had once felt in my heart had now seeped its way into my body, for now everything ached. Nothing was worse than the pounding of my head, and hearing a voice now made it ever the more difficult to concentrate.

"Sir, I'm afraid Milady will be awake soon, and I know not what she will think when she finds you did not sleep in your bed." Hearing this certainly brought me back to my senses, and this included remembering the events of the night before. Hence, why my eyes snapped opened and suddenly I jumped to my feet. I did so too quickly, needing to hold out my hand to brace myself, for I could feel the room spinning around me making me nearly knock over one of my mother's prized vases, one her dear John had given her yet again.

My damn brother.

"Yes alright, I thank you, Bess." The dear woman gave me a smile, and it was of little wonder considering I was the only person in this godforsaken household that was nice to her, other than the other servants, of course. Questioning my family's morals and common decency was something that I had done many times before, for it often made me give thought as to where I myself had come from.

My late father perhaps, for he most certainly had a kinder constitution than that of my mother. I often wondered, when listening to the monotonous sermons at church, what exactly it was my father had done to offend Christ himself to end up with such a woman. In fact, it was through these very musings that I first formed within myself a determination never to enter into matrimony for anything other than love.

Something I had only yesterday foolishly believed myself to be in. However, last night had proven me wrong and made me now question everything. My mother was always trying to push upon on me women she believed of consequence, which was another term for what title she held and how much money her family possessed. For in truth, my mother wouldn't have cared if the woman being presented to me resembled a suckling pig, as long as the apple in its mouth was golden.

I had to confess, these last few weeks in pursuing the affections of Margaret, had made me feel alive for the first time in a long time. But then, I had always felt out of place, and felt myself stumbling through the building bricks of life wondering when they would just come tumbling down around me, caging me in. I so wished to be free. I longed to travel and see the world and I envied those that were lucky enough to do so. I had wanted to join the regiment or take to the seas in the Royal Navy, but of course mother wouldn't allow this. No, alas, I was to become a solicitor or join the clergy, and considering listening to sermons bored me to tears, I could very well imagine that having to be the one to deliver them would have sent me across the edge of madness.

So, I did what most men did in my position and joined a firm and worked within the realms of the law, and in truth, I was sick of it all. Of course, I often felt somewhat guilty, for there are far more than I who would wish for a different life and, unlike most, I was not living in slums and starving on the streets. And whereas my mother and my brother would have cast their noses up along with their judgments against those born to such unfortunate a circumstance, I would not. No, instead I would often give them a coin or two, feeling slightly less guilty at the fact that they could at least feed themselves and last for that little bit longer before starvation took life.

I didn't know why it grieved me so, but it did. Just knowing of so many people that were living a life of hunger and on the streets, and yet here I was, in the life of luxury, complaining that I was not free to do as I pleased. In truth, our circumstances were painted as thus, for I was a well-fed bird in a beautiful, gilded cage, and one forced to look upon the world through bars protected by the money that surrounded me. And the rest of the world were birds that were free to roam the skies to do and go wherever they pleased. However, the price of this was to find their own way in the world, not knowing where their next meal would come from or when the next predator would strike.

Surely there was somewhere in between?

For surely there was someone out there that lived the balance of the two and if they did, well, I was yet to meet them, and no doubt should such a perchance ever happen, I would feel the bitter sting of jealousy when I did.

The moment I heard the bell ring was my distinct signal to leave and Bessie knew it, which is why she said to me,

"If it pleases, my Lord, may I suggest a walk... after all, it is said to do wonders after too much whiskey and water." I scoffed a laugh and nodded.

"Perhaps you are right. Besides, if my mother wakes and discovers me here, smelling like a distillery, she may start locking away the liquor." I whispered this last part, making Bessie laugh, before going off to fetch my coat and hat.

As for me, I looked down at myself and tried to make the best of what it was after spending the night sleeping in my clothes. However, I knew there was no chance of me going to change and not encountering the old hag. Someone, I should hasten to mention, who didn't have a maternal bone in her body and made this fact well known. For she believed that children were to be unseen and unheard until they had turned into an adult and had something useful to say. Needless to mention, this did not exactly warm me to my mother in any way, shape nor form. As for my brother John, he saw things quite differently, but then again, he always did when coin was involved.

Inheritance was everything to John, as he would keep reminding me, and keeping the old woman sweet was part of this. But then, someone had to pay for his gambling and his whores.

"It is perhaps best we not mention this to my mother." Bessie knew instantly what I was asking, and she tapped her nose like she always did when she knew she needed to keep quiet about certain things.

"If she asks of you, Sir?"

"Tell her I left for work early and explain how I'll be home late." She grinned and nodded her head about to leave me to go on my way, when the oddest thing happened, she stopped me suddenly and said,

"If I may be so bold, Sir, perhaps a walk towards the park would be well advised."

"Oh?"

"I hear there might be something unexpected going on

there today." After this she bowed a little and left, leaving me questioning her meaning. It was true Bessie usually spoke freely around me, for Christ knew that she couldn't in front of anyone else in my family. But I had never seen her speak so seriously, as if she was trying to tell me something, yet the cryptic words she found were all she was allowed to say.

I released a sigh and tucked down the brim of my hat, deciding to take her advice, knowing I wasn't the of sort to hold weight to superstition, for I never wanted to ask myself, what if? I never wanted to question actions I myself might have been able to change. After all, you could not change the actions of others for they were out of your control, but at the very least you could do was take claim for your own.

So, with this in mind, I headed down the steps and onto the street, heading a way I knew would lead me to the park that the house overlooked. It didn't take more than a few footsteps for the fog of drink to clear from my head. I didn't wish to think back to last night's events, but I confess it was difficult not to.

How could I have been so blind and so enamoured? So much so that I failed to see the truth. She had dangled me like a fish on a hook and teased me with the river. I wondered then how long it would have been before I would have been tossed aside to the banks of the Thames and have her discard my love, no doubt just like many before me. Possibly when my accounts had run dry, and my creditors were chasing me all over London. Perhaps when my pockets were no longer full of the coins and my hand empty of gifts.

What a fickle creature indeed.

I was only thankful that I had not taken that last step to discredit my own honour when foolishly believing it was hers that I was maintaining. But clearly it was an honour she had tossed away long ago every time she lifted her skirts and invited someone in between her legs.

But I didn't want a whore, and if I did, I knew many a place to go and get one for the night. Many would have called me a sentimental old fool, despite claiming the age of two and thirty. A man of my age that should be married off by now and creating offspring for the family name, as my mother liked to remind me any chance she got. But, like I said, I wasn't interested in a town's prized cow put up for auction. As if claiming the heart was just merely another trade to be taken advantage of. Another form of currency to hand over to the highest bidder.

I found it all rather distasteful to be honest and wondered when the world would ever change. Of course, there were those that married for love, but they were far and few between, especially when found to be a gentleman. And those that did marry beneath them, doing so for love, were often shunned, and cast out like tarnished silver that could not be cleaned of their sins. But marrying for love was not a sin in my mind.

Marrying for love was one of life's greatest gifts, and one that I was determinedly setting out to discover and gain for myself.

For love was… currently a woman stepping out in front of an uncontrollable carriage!

What felt like the woman of my dreams was about to…

Die!

ELEVEN

TURTLE DOVE

"**L**ook out!"

I shouted in vain for it was too late. All I managed to do was to prevent her from continuing on and perhaps having a chance at missing the carriage, for suddenly the beautiful woman stopped and stared at me. I glanced at the carriage getting closer and acted on impulse. This meant that I ran towards her and threw myself into her body. I took the poor girl off her feet and tried to cushion her landing with my arms around her. I knew such an aggressive action would have no doubt hurt her but at the very least she was breathing, and right then that was all I cared for. The reactions of others were lost and became an unimportant element, as I felt the soft curves of a woman beneath the length of me. I had landed fully on top of her slight frame that was now caged in my arms in hopes of protecting her.

As for the carriage, I vaguely heard its destruction with the crunching of metal and snapping of wood as clearly it had come to an untimely end. But I had no concern left over for that, nor for its rider or any victims it may have taken, for selfishly, everything in my entire being was far too consumed and taken up by the woman beneath me.

I pulled back enough so as I may take in the sight of her face, and this time, the beauty I saw there staring back at me was unlike any other I had ever seen before.

She was utterly captivating.

In fact, I questioned my sanity for she didn't seem real. Her skin looked so soft I almost found myself reaching out to touch it in fear my hand would pass straight through such a vision. Her hair was a colour I had never seen before, for it was red but not the usual orange tone, more like the colour of a shiny red apple or cherry. It made me want to remove the delicate little velvet hat she wore just so I could see her curls cascading down her beautiful face.

But this wasn't the most incredible feature she held, no, that was reserved solely for her eyes. Large eyes that were looking up at me now in wonder. The only way to describe them was where land met the sea, for they were the forest and water combined. A green so lush and vibrant she could have been mistaken for some forest goddess that commanded nature. But the blue in them, was the colour of sapphires.

Everything else about her was considered simply lovely, and sweet and there was a kindness there that could not be denied. It was why the first words out of my lips were ones never spoken to another before. For it was as if they had solely been reserved for her in my heart.

"Turtle Dove," I whispered, making her suddenly beam up at me, as if my endearment had meant just as much to her hearing it as it did to me having reason in saying it. But then, as if she wanted to hear it again, she spoke, and I found myself glad of it, for her voice was almost as enchanting as the rest of her.

"Excuse me, Sir?" she said in a sweet, harmonious tone. A voice that I confessed I could have listened to all day and never grown tired of such a beauty. I felt as if I was in some sort of trance or caught in a spell that she had unknowingly cast upon me. It felt so strong that it caused me to physically shake my head a moment, as if to rid myself of it before I was able to form such a response. One, this time, that was more befitting of a gentleman.

Hence, why I forced myself to move, despite the pain it caused by putting distance between us. But it was clear we had grown quite a bit of attention as a crowd was starting to form. One muttering about the events that had just passed. So, as I gained my feet, I held out my hand to her to aid her to her own.

"Madame, please forgive me, are you well?" I said as she placed her gloved hand in mine, and I marvelled at how light she was when lifting her easily to her feet. Then when she seemed to stumble a little, I reached out and steadied her with my hand to her side. Her reaction to this was a peculiar one as she actually giggled. This was before whispering one word, barely even caught by my own ears despite how close I was. But in this one word she gave reason to her reaction, and I found it the most endearing one, along with the sound she had made.

"Ticklish."

I couldn't help but grin down at her, marvelling at how little she was, for it suddenly made me incredibly protective over her. In fact, the most insane urge came over me and I wanted nothing more than to toss her over my shoulder like some Neanderthal and run away with her back to my cave. She barely came up to my chest and I could have spanned her dainty waist with my large hands.

"I am quite well, Sir, I assure you, thanks to you of course. I am greatly indebted to you." Good lord but I actually felt myself blushing after being given such praise. I removed my hat, one surprisingly I had not lost in the fray, and told her the truth of my feelings.

"Not at all, my Lady, my happiness lies in knowing you are well and unharmed in this matter but… where is your escort?" I asked, enquiring this last part whilst looking around and praying that in doing so, I didn't come across a husband or that of an already chosen suitor. But then she shocked me.

"I am afraid you find me quite alone, Sir. I have lost my way and along with it my escort." Lost her way indeed. Well, I could not be happier for it, as it had led the little lamb my way and I was not about to give up such a gift such as this, nor the opportunity. But first I needed to be sure.

"Your husband must not be so lax in his duties, my

Lady, and I feel, as a gentleman, I must have his name to rectify this matter and inform him at once. For a Lady of your great beauty is not safe alone, least of all on the streets of town," I said in a firmer tone, allowing my hatred for such a man to coat my words of distaste. For no husband should allow such a thing to happen.

But then, in truth, my distaste had not been solely born from the man's carelessness or his failings, but more from the idea of the man himself and having the right to claim this gorgeous creature as his wife.

Christ in Heaven, but even the idea of another man touching her would have been enough to send me into a murderous rage. One that would have knocking out that simple minded brute last night seem like child's roughhousing. No, it would have been nothing compared to what I would have done, should I have seen another man taking what I claim to be in my heart as my own. It may have seemed like folly to make such a claim, but I could not help it and nor would I want to, for this woman before me felt like mine and mine alone.

But then, before I allowed these murderous thoughts to fully take hold, she granted me with yet another gift.

"I have no husband, Sir, for in which to beseech." My

head quickly whipped back down to look at her, and my next question was out of my mouth before I could prevent it.

"A fiancé then?" I hated even the very sound of it and I knew if it was true, I would do everything in my power to make sure that whoever this person was would not stay her fiancé for long. But then just as before, she continued to bestow on me all the right gifts that were leading me to believe I would be free to claim her as my own after I wooed her and captured her heart as she had already done with my own.

"Alas no, Sir."

"Not even betrothed?" I asked as the very last hurdle that could potentially stand in my way, caring little for my eager tone.

"No, Sir," she answered, lowering her face, one that I could see now was blushing. I would perhaps have felt guilty from enticing such a reaction from her, and feeling as though I had put her in an uncomfortable situation conversing with me as such. And, had it not been for two factors in play, that guilt would have taken hold. For the beguiling tone of blush that graced her heavenly skin strangely made me feel as if I wanted to growl. As if I

wanted to nip at it, kiss it, lick it and last of all bite it, like the elusive forbidden apple from the tree of Eden. Because that's exactly what she was, for I didn't care whether it condemned my soul to Hell for all of eternity, it was one I would stop at nothing for until I had tasted.

My golden apple.

And of course, the small smile that graced her lips was another reason I didn't feel guilt that from my brazen actions, as I had been the one to put it there.

"In that case, please allow me to escort you home, my Lady," I said, holding my arm out to her, waiting for hers to be placed in the crook of my own, so I may keep it there with my own hand covering it. Of course, my main aim in being able to escort her back to her home was so I would know where she lived, and therefore could try and learn all there was to know about her. But first there was one thing left unsaid and unknown. One that I needed almost as much as the touch she bestowed upon me with her dainty little hand held under mine.

"May I be so bold as to enquire after your name, my Lady?" The sweet dear girl looked up at me with those big green and blue eyes of hers as she smiled. I swear the sight forced me to swallow hard, for the explicit and sexual nature of my thoughts started running riot in my mind. Thoughts that were barely containable, for all I wanted to do now was grace that smile with a kiss.

But my sweet girl was the gift that continued to keep giving for she gave me her name, one I couldn't wait to whisper from my own lips.

"Certainly, Sir, I am Miss Winifred Ambrogetti and you Sir, pray, what would you have me call you?" she asked in return, licking her lips and rendering me mute for the seemingly innocent action had gone straight to my cock. In the end, I realised that I had been staring at those lips for far too long and found myself having to clear my throat first before finding my voice. One that was barely warranted as being of importance, for it merely made me look like a fool when needing to ask her to repeat her question.

"Umm... oh, yes... forgive me, what was your question?" She laughed in that sweet musical voice of hers, and I decided from that moment on to make it my personal mission to hear this sound as much as possible and to be the cause of it.

Her laugh was beautiful.

It was enticing and endearing, and made you smile and feel better off for hearing it. I was quickly making a very long list indeed of my favourite attributes about her, but I had to confess that her laugh had quickly jumped to the top. Along with that innocent licking of her lips, that looked naturally red and plump and substantial enough to feel soft beneath my own. But then, I could see she had a mischievous side, for she once again sucked in her bottom lip, holding it captive between her teeth as if trying to entice me to do the same. I took in a deep breath and felt it release again on a shudder.

Christ almighty, she had the ability to completely undo me and render me barely able to function as a gentleman around her.

I wanted to fucking ravish her!

"Your name, Sir?" she asked again after releasing her lip, and doing so slowly as if to tempt me even further, *the little minx*. I wanted to punish her for it in the best way possible and one that she would beg me for. I barely knew where these carnal thoughts were coming from... no, that wasn't true. I knew exactly where they were coming from.

Winifred.

The name suited her well, but my little Winnie suited her better.

"Ah, but of course, how rude of me. I am Mr Adam

Fitzwilliam of Westenbury, at your service Miss Winifred."
She giggled again at this, and I found myself grinning down at her. She was so little, she made me feel like a giant. But then I thought on her last name and to keep conversation flowing, I inquired after her unusual family name, for I wanted to know all there was to know about her.

"Ambrogetti? That is the most unusual name."

"It's Greek, Sir, and I believe it means 'Immortal'." Hearing this, and not only did it make me wish for an eternity with her, but I also found it quite fitting. For she was like one of those Greek goddesses of beauty you read about in books.

For in truth, it felt as if she had been....

Sent to me by the Gods.

STEPHANIE HUDSON

TWELVE

MY SNEAKY LITTLE IMP
PRESENT DAY

I couldn't help but grin when thinking back to that day. Of course, knowing what I knew now, then I had no other option than to be amused by it, especially when discovering that Lucius had been the one controlling the runaway carriage and that Pip was, in actual fact, never in any real danger.

So how could I be angry at the ruse? How could I be angry knowing that she had been there that night and only helped me discover the foolish mistakes I was making. I thought back to that woman I had stupidly fallen for and one I could barely remember the name of, or at least I would have forgot entirely... if my naughty little Imp didn't constantly remind me of the indisputable mistakes I had made in believing myself in love with her.

Margaret Defoe.

I had no clue why I had been so infatuated with her, but it all seemed so ridiculous the moment I found my woman beneath me on that street floor. My fated love. Suddenly, all thoughts of Margaret had left me in an instant, and not because of the hurt she had inflicted on me the night before. I would never forget what my feelings had been in that moment when gazing upon Winnie's face. That look of wonder staring up at me after I foolishly believed I had saved her life.

By the Gods did I love my Imp.

My little Winnie.

In fact, I remember thinking it would have been impossible to love her any more than I had in that moment, as I had quickly fallen for her charms the very second we met. But then, in this, I would have been wrong, because every moment after that, my feelings for her only grew stronger, and even to this day I could not claim the impossibility. Because my love for her never stopped growing.

Current actions notwithstanding, of course.

But now there was nothing to stand in our way from being together, which was a good job, considering there would have been a lot of casualties since being combined with my beast, had anyone been crazy enough to try and take her from me. I could only imagine what the fallout of such a thing would be.

My beast knew, of course.

He had made it perfectly clear on those same feelings the moment we were united, just as the Gods had intended. I felt his pain of having her ripped away from him and his great sadness and loss when discovering her taken. And then I'd had but a glimpse of the utter rage that had consumed him as he had tried to tear Hell apart looking for her. And meanwhile, during the time this was all happening to him, I was happily spending my time as a mortal and becoming totally enraptured by the beauty. One that was the cause of such pain and destruction for the Beast below. But I knew she must have found this so hard. Not only to leave him but to know that he would not again settle or be at ease until she could find him a host.

To be honest, it was the very reason that the moment

Abaddon was joined to my soul, he knew this was his one and only opportunity to be able to continue life with Pip. He needed me and for me to have an eternal life with her, I also needed him, because that was what always centred the two of us living as one…

Our combined love for Pip.

But despite this and the lies I knew she was forced to tell me, I only looked back at our time together with nothing but fond memories. Memories that were filled with a hope in my heart that bloomed daily whenever she was in it.

That was until the day I foolishly introduced her to…

My mother.

12TH OCTOBER 1680

After the accident, and what could have been a grave and disastrous end, I escorted miss Winifred to where she said her uncle would be waiting for her. Of course, I couldn't be too cross when meeting the man. Not after she had admitted the fault was her own after travelling too far from her escort and getting lost in the process. No, in truth, I actually found myself glad of it, for had she not done so I would never have had the life changing pleasure of meeting her.

Alas, we met her uncle in a well-known coffee house called the Grecian. One that held its central location in Devereux Court, off Fleet Street. I knew it well for it was often frequented by lawyers and solicitors alike. Of course, the coffee house had changed somewhat since first appearing, for I would often recall my father grumbling about them not being the most reputable of places to be seen in. However, things had vastly changed since and now they were ideal venues for socialising, and debates on trade gossip and conducting business. As for the Grecian, it had been there for three years and every time I had found myself with an urge for coffee and local gossip to be heard, I had come here and found it busy.

"Pray tell me, what is it your uncle does?" I asked, curious to know.

"He's a land owner, Sir." This was all she said before I was meeting this uncle of hers, and I had to say it was a surprising acquaintance. He was barely, if at all, any older than me!

However, with this being said, I liked him. He seemed

appalled at the idea of what could have befallen his niece, and gently took her in his arms to embrace her. I liked that he didn't care what others around him believed to be inappropriate, for in this we were of the same mind and sentiment

Then he shook my hand and thanked me, telling me I was welcome in his home at any time. He also openly told me that he felt strongly about my character. This was proven not to be an empty falsehood, as I enquired to call upon his niece the next day. To which he had whole heartedly given his consent and what's more, without an escort!

However, when I had questioned this to Miss Winifred the very next day we met, she laughed it off and with a wave of her dainty hand.

"He is not originally from these parts, although his English would convince you otherwise. No, where he is from, they are far less reserved and uninhibited from modern convention. Should we say... he lives a more free life and basically does as he pleases, caring little for what others think of him," she had said, smiling.

"I have to confess I feel rather jealous," I had admitted.

"Sir?"

"To have that kind of freedom, well I believe it to be what many would truly wish for, should they be brave enough to confess such." It was at that moment we stopped walking on the cobbled streets when she placed slight pressure on my arm. Then she had boldly asked me,

"And you, Fitzwilliam, what do you wish for?" That sweet voice of hers, it was one that she had no idea was as enticing and alluring as it was. For it made me want to slice open my chest and bear all of my inner secrets to her. Every single one, until they came pouring out of me, spilling from my heart. However, seeing as I had only met her yesterday and granted, under unusual circumstance, I did not yet feel confident to do so. I knew many would have called me a fool for believing myself so in love after just one perchance meeting, and although I cared little for what others would say on the matter, what I did care for were her own thoughts. And, until I could be sure of them, I was not going to allow for my heart to get ahead of my mind and risk losing her. No, first I wanted her to fall as madly in love with me as I had with her and until I was assured of that, I would continue to act like the gentleman that was expected of me.

Which brought me back to my need to answer her.

"Right now, I wish to take you for some hot chocolate."

"Chocolate?" she asked with an adorable little wrinkle to her nose, as it was clear she had never even heard of the word. I decided this was a great opportunity to see if I could get away with playfully teasing her, for I had the feeling that she was mischievous enough to enjoy it.

"Upon my word, I am surprised, for someone as sweet as you surely has heard of the best kept secret in London." At this, her eyes sparkled with mirth and that smile grew.

"I have been away too long, for clearly there are things in London that I most definitely have been missing out on, along with its company," she answered, licking her lips and again making it hard to continue to be a gentleman. Especially when all I wanted to do was pull her up against me and back her into an alleyway before tasting those lips for myself. But it wasn't just the enticing action or the way her lips glistened, now after being lavished with her tongue, one I most decidedly wanted to duel with. But alas, it was also her words, being of such they were almost considered a declaration that what she had missed in London had been the opportunity to meet me. I tried not to read too much into it, but I had to confess the hope was hard to extinguish.

"Then come, for you will give me the great honour of being the first to introduce you to such a delicacy." At this, she beamed up at me and then patted the crook of my arm where her hand rested and said,

"Very well, lead on, Columbus, and we will discover this marvel of the new world, together." At this I couldn't help it, but I burst out laughing for her humour was unlike any I had ever known. It was freeing and enlightening and made what felt like my whole body come alive!

Because being with her made me feel like that bird that could soar to the skies despite the dangers.

For with her, I knew deep down that I could finally…

Live and love freely.

STEPHANIE HUDSON

THIRTEEN

SWEET TEMPTATIONS

"I promise you, Sir, I have never experienced this chocolate you claim to be life changing," Winifred said, with merriment in her eyes making them glisten like wet jewels. As for her tone, it was of a teasing sort, and it lightened my heart to hear of it.

"Then come and let me change your world for the better, for the sight of your smile certainly has had that a same effect on me and it has barely been a day," I said, going back on my word and being too hasty with my sentiments. However, I quickly learned through her reaction to it that it was not a mistake made. For she blushed and granted me a soft smile before telling me,

"You do me great honour by complimenting me thus."

"Ah, but it is you that compliments me, by gracing me with your beautiful presence on my arm," I told her gently so she may hear the depths of sincerity in my words. Her blush deepened and she smiled at the cobbled streets as we continued to walk.

Thankfully, we weren't far away from Bishopsgate as I headed to the first chocolate house in Queens Head alley. It was said that a Frenchman had opened the premises luring in Londoners with the promise of an excellent West Indian drink. I had to confess, the luxury had lived up to the claim, for it was indeed delicious, and one I was eager to share with Winifred.

"My word, it must be good for it surely looks busy," she commented, as I opened the door for her to enter and we stood in line ready to be served. But then, as people made their way past us I found myself thankful for the crush of bodies, as it presented me with the excuse to act upon what I wanted to do the most, which was get closer to her. I found my arms going around her in a protective manner and she sucked in a quick breath, telling me that she was not immune to the physical foundations of my affections.

It now made me wonder what being married to this delightful creature would be like. I had heard many depressing tales of a husband finding his pleasures at some brothel, because his wife had considered the carnal acts as merely a duty to produce an heir to continue generations of a family name. I heard tales of separate bedrooms just like my own parents had. But now, looking down at my little Winnie, I knew I could never allow something like that to be possible. For if I finally ever got her in my bed, I knew with a certainty that I would never want her out of it again. For the idea of spending a night apart was utter abhorrent to me and not to be heard of.

But then I could not help myself questioning whether it was the combined vision of her blushing skin or the wide eyes now looking up at me that made me act, for I could not stop my hand from reaching out and brushing back a single curl that had sprung free and was now resting next to her eye.

"Thank you," she said sweetly, and I nodded my head down at her, silently communicating that she was most welcome. She was so very sweet. In truth, I didn't actually know where this side of me had come from, but it was as if being around her gave me such a confidence I would act without thought. I would be the man that I had always dreamed of being around a woman.

I would have scoffed aloud at the memory of the bumbling idiot I had been around Margaret and now I questioned why. Perhaps that was more of an indication of how wrong such a union would have been. Perhaps it was a way for my mind to tell me that something wasn't right, yet my heart decided not to listen. Well, both were communicating well enough now and doing so by working harmoniously together, for when I was with Winifred, nothing had ever felt so right.

After this close moment shared between us, we unfortunately had to separate due to the line in front of us now becoming clear. I therefore placed the order and paid for our drinks, before we spotted a free table by the window.

"I will go and secure the table whilst you carry the drinks," she offered and then stepped away from me. I felt my hands clench into fists just to stop myself from reaching out and grabbing her. I had the insane urge not to let her out of my reach, for fear that some harm would befall upon her. In fact, what stopped me, was the knowledge that it would have been an almost certain judgement cast from her eyes, should I have been so bold as to do so. A thought that prevented me of the compulsion. So, instead, I took our cups and walked over to the table, doing so quickly now so she was not left there alone for long.

"Be careful," I warned, making her raise a brow in question. Then I was bold enough to take the cup from her hands so I could raise it to my lips. Then, without taking my eyes from hers, I blew across the chocolate liquid, before explaining,

"It is hot." The look she gave me was one I couldn't place, but if I was to venture a guess, I would say that my actions had meant something to her. However, instead of granting me her real feelings she teased back,

"Hence the name." Then with a smile, she took the cup from my hands and took over blowing on the hot liquid. I couldn't explain it, but every time we touched, and our skin came into contact, it was as if I was being jolted into feeling something buzzing inside of me. As though up until this moment I had been a mere shell, walking through the motions of life and really unseeing, unhearing, and unfeeling of everything around me. And now in walked this being so full of life she was transferring it into my very own, as it felt as though I was experiencing everything for the first time all over again.

It was exhilarating!

And speaking of exhilarating, the moment the hot chocolate was cool enough for her to drink, she took a tentative sip and the way her eyes shot to mine and widened, made me chuckle. That childlike innocence was adorable and as I took a sip of my own, it was once again as if I was experiencing life for a second time.

"Do you like it?" I asked, knowing the answer already from her reaction. Yet, in truth, it was just an excuse to hear her voice and to witness her enjoyment through her own words.

"Like it, I fear I will never get enough of it! It is exquisite, the sweetness bursts against my tongue yet it is a taste I've never experienced before... will you be drinking all of yours do you think?" At this I laughed, and said to her,

"I will buy you another, sweetheart." On hearing this endearment, she blushed and grinned to herself as she continued to drink. Although, I had to confess my amusement didn't just come from her expression, but more in the way she kept glancing at my own cup to gauge how much of it was left. I couldn't help myself, for trying to hide my own grin was the hardest part as I tested the theory. Doing so for the sole purpose of discovering what her eyes might say whenever I took a sip of my own. She looked so disappointed whenever I drank from my own cup, that I nearly choked on it, although I had to confess, the sight was an endearingly funny one. In the end, just because I wanted to see the smile on her face and with over half a cup left, I pushed it her way and said,

"Why don't you finish that whilst I go and get us some more." Her beautiful eyes lighting up for me was reward enough, and I swear, by the time this occasion would end, I would be ready to buy the whole damn shop and gift it to her. She looked very touched by such a meagre offering and my heart soared.

I knew at that moment I had to go and get more, or I would have stayed and kissed her, damning both of our reputations. Of course, I found it difficult to tear my eyes away from her, even when across the other side the shop and waiting for the chocolatey liquid to be poured.

I was eager to get back to her and paid for them quickly. However, once I sat down, and handed hers to her, she asked me,

"Are they expensive?" I shook my head as I didn't want to discuss how much they were, yet this was something she clearly didn't want to let go of.

"How much?" she asked with a nod of her head to prompt me, and I found I could not deny her an answer. So, I told her the price. Her eyes grew wide, and her reaction was a curious one, for here she sat, dressed in the finest of green silk and lace, and just as her uncle had been, I knew she was not short of such luxuries, for surely, she was accustomed to such. But then her reaction surprised me.

"Such a luxury, and such an expense."

"No expense is too great to ensure your happiness," I told her but once again she shocked me to my core.

"I do not believe that happiness is gained through all that you possess. Don't misunderstand my meaning, gifts are beautiful and lovely to receive, as are reminders of affection that is held between two people. However, I find words work just as well, if not better for they are not bought but are of the expense of the heart and therefore more worth the earning." At this I could do little else but stare at her, now utterly dumbfounded! But then, as if my reaction did not look as shocking as it felt, she continued to grant me her thoughts.

"For I do so wish to marry a man for love and not for financial gain or family status. In truth, my honest opinion is that I believe love is the source of all happiness, and that happiness is gained by spending your time with the right person…" she said, taking but a moment to drink some more before she once again continued as if now utterly lost to her thoughts, and I found myself captivated by them.

"…and if that should be in something you could barely consider a home, then that would still make you the richest person alive, and one far richer than living with the wrong man without love, under the luxuries of a palace. But then I know my thoughts on the matter are most likely considered outrageous and controversial." I couldn't help it, but in that moment I felt my hand reaching for her and taking possession of it. Then my fingers tightened around her own, taking care not to do so in a hurtful manner but one that just expressed how deeply her thoughts and feelings had affected me.

"Turtle dove." I whispered my affectionate endearment for her, for I couldn't help it, nor could I help the way I gripped her tightly and pulled her closer to me. I wished suddenly that we were not out in the open amongst people, but somewhere secluded. Somewhere just for us.

Somewhere that no prying eyes of society could judge us, and we could have but just one moment to ourselves in our own world we had just created.

"Fitzwilliam?" she said my name, but it didn't feel intimate enough.

"Adam, please call me Adam, for I so long to hear the sound of my name being graced by your lips."

"Oh, Adam," she uttered, and I swear I had to close my eyes, for the whole force of my being felt as if it were to burst from my skin, as if there was a beast within me that was pushing me to claim her. I had never wanted nor craved something so much in all of my life, and by God I vowed that I would one day have her. That I may one day keep her until death do us part.

"If you please, may I be so bold as to trouble you with a request," I asked, feeling my voice thick and full of feeling.

"It is no trouble, as I would do anything for you," she said quickly, making me suck in a startled breath at the admission. Her eyes turned wide and this time, her blush was out of embarrassment through her own doing. It was breath-taking.

"I'm sorry, that was very bold of me," she said, and I

had to swallow hard before finding my voice once more.

"Please do not apologise, for I assure you that your words were taken as they were hopefully intended, and therefore meant a great deal to me." At this she smiled, and it was near blinding before she placed her hands in front of her on the table, and said,

"Oh good, then feel free to ask away. I am all ears that await your handsome voice." Again, her admission shocked me, and I must have shown such on my face once more. She gasped and covered her lips.

"I'm sorry, I've done it again, haven't I?" I laughed and shook my head a little as if this would help in answering whether this moment was real or not.

"It must be the chocolate, pray tell me, does it have the same effect as alcohol, for that would explain it?" I smirked and ended up having to bite the bottom of my own lip before answering her.

"I confess, I am greatly relieved that it doesn't have any effect on a person's mind or their endearing behaviour," I said, making her question,

"You're relieved?"

"Miss Winifred, if you don't already know by now, I greatly enjoy your company, but even more so when you speak freely and without fear of being ridiculed, for it is something I can assure you I would never do." At this, she granted me such a smile it transformed her whole face into something glorious, for it was obvious I had made her happy in my response.

"So, you wish me to speak plainly, no matter how shocking… you still wish to know my mind, for I'd better warn you, sometimes my lips speak before my mind tells me to think better of it," she admitted, making me laugh a little.

"Then I looked forward to hearing what your lips have to say without your mind interfering." At this, she blushed again as she leaned over the table to get closer to me. Then she beckoned me even closer with a jerk of her two fingers.

This was when she had my heart quickening as she confessed on a shocking whisper,

"I find you very handsome." On hearing this, I felt myself now being the one to blush and I raised a brow.

"Is that so?" I forced out of my lips, which was not easy considering I could not contain the grin from them. She did not answer with words this time but instead with the mirth in her eyes and a quick nod of her head telling me that yes, she did.

"Then may I tell you something in return?" I said in a mischievous tone of my own.

"Oh, please do, maybe we could make it a secret, that way it will make it so much more exciting," she said, playfully clapping her hands in front of her and making me laugh.

"I wish we could make it a secret, but unfortunately this is a claim that I make as one I would be willing to shout from the very rooftops of the highest building London has." Now this time she looked shy and even more lovely.

"And that is?" she asked in a quiet voice.

"That I find you the most beautiful and captivating creature I've ever beheld," I told her, now being just as bold as she and feeling elevated from it. I could have said more… I wanted to say more but I decided that I would lead from her example, so, I would wait.

"Really, you find me beautiful?" she asked, making me jerk back a little as I was shocked.

"But of course, for surely you must agree with me on such a thing for you must possess a mirror." She laughed and then reached out and gripped my hand surprising me once again.

"You are very kind. In truth, I never considered myself

beautiful, although I do like the colour of my eyes."

"As do I, very much so, for I am starting to think that my new favourite colours are both forest green and sapphire blue." At this, her eyes widened awarding me more of them.

"Mine too!" she shouted, gaining us quite a few looks from other customers. She covered her mouth and giggled behind her hand as she looked at them and then back at me, as if she had made an amusing mistake.

"But wait, I am afraid that we went off topic as I do believe you were going to ask me something before my shocking behaviour," she asked in a teasing tone, and I knew that the moment had come for me to take our relationship to the next step,

When I told her...

"I would like you to meet my mother."

FOURTEEN

DISAPPROVAL BE DAMNED
16TH OCTOBER 1680

Upon reflection, having her meet my mother so soon was most likely a bad idea. However, I knew she was the only and last obstacle that stood in my way from asking for Winifred's hand in marriage. That and, of course, approaching her uncle with the same notion.

But I had convinced myself that all my mother cared about was that she had a big enough dowry and a family name, and to be honest, I had not yet been assured of either for personally I cared little. In truth, I had been too busy spending every waking moment thinking of her, that I had little thought left for anything else. Then again, the moments in the evening were no different, for I would dream of her being mine and cursed myself upon the morning light.

I had been desperate to see her again and it pained me that it had been three whole days since the last time, as business had taken me from town and back to our country estate of Westenbury. Something that, had we been married, I would have ensured she travelled with me. But of course to do so now, or to even offer such, would have been inappropriate to most. It would have been classed as too hasty and not proper of an English gentleman. Besides, I doubt her uncle would have agreed, no matter how lax he was concerning his niece spending time with a man and unaccompanied by an escort.

However, this wasn't to say that I had not learned an awful lot about Miss Ambrogetti. This was by her own admission when I inquired after her family during our journey back from Queens Head Valley. In truth, it was conversations like this that should have happened at the beginning of my first meeting with her. But, I had to say I was so captivated and lost in those green blue eyes of hers that we could have spoken about anything, and I would have clung to every word she said.

However, this time my question was, for once, one that prompted a reply I did not relish in hearing.

"I am without family, Sir."

"Adam, please," I urged her in a soft tone as I could see the sadness in her eyes.

"Adam," she said in a warm affectionate tone before continuing on.

"I have my uncle, of course, but he is my only family left."

"I am sorry to hear that, my Winnie," I said, calling her this for the first time aloud, for it had been said many a time in my mind before. However, the sadness in her face vanished and therefore I knew it was worth allowing the slip of my tongue.

"Your Winnie?" she questioned, and I shrugged my shoulders for I was not going to lie and take it back. I would not do that to her. So, instead, I stopped her from taking another step and turned her round to face me. This was when I admitted the truth as I ran the backs of two fingers down her sweet, heated face, one that was once again blushing,

"Yes, my Winnie, for it is my hope that it will one

day…"

"Yes?" she asked, not being able to bear the patience for the pause I took, eager to have the rest of my claim and it gave me enough strength to continue to make it,

"That one day it will be made so under the eyes of God." At this her response was an unusual one as she said happily,

"Well, I believe that to have already happened, for here we are now." She didn't add anything more to this odd reply and I didn't question it, for I was too busy relishing in the happiness in her eyes that only gave strength to her words.

"Winnie, I…" It was in this moment that my declaration of love was cut short, as a carriage came too close to us and made it so that we had to move to one side. This then meant that the moment was lost.

After such, as we continued to walk back to where I knew her uncle would be meeting her once more. I discovered that her parents had died, and she was now under the charge and guardianship of her uncle. She spoke about this freely and openly. And when I asked her if she missed them, she answered that there had only been one being she had really classed as family, and yes, she had been heartbroken to lose him.

Unfortunately, this was when our journey and our conversation ended, for we had arrived. Leaving me with only the hope that this male she missed so very much had been a brother of hers and no one that had claimed her heart before I myself could claim it first.

At the very least, I knew I would have more time to ask, as we arranged a time for them both to come and meet with my mother. Unfortunately, this was not to be any sooner than three days after, for I knew I had business to attend that took me from town.

As for the meeting with my mother well, needless to say, it had not gone half as well as I had hoped. In fact, I found myself utterly embarrassed by my mother's behaviour, and her comments about sin and foreigners made me now want to strangle her myself.

Thankfully, my lovely Winnie didn't look as if she had taken any heed to my mother's snide remarks and instead, I would find her smirking behind her hand. Then, whenever she caught me staring at her, she would wink at me as if trying to offer me comfort from the clear distress that could be seen across my features. It had been in the moment that they were about to leave when I found myself standing and forcing myself to stay in place, for I had wanted to go to her so badly. I had wanted to apologise for everything my mother had said and the way she had acted, but I knew it would have only made the situation worse. So, I forced myself to remain stood on the spot after her uncle had declared it time for them to take their leave.

"Mrs Fitzwilliam, Mr Fitzwilliam, it was a pleasure, but we must now take our leave, good day to you both." I thought this at least be my excuse to go to her, but as I opened my mouth, I barely got out a few words before I was interrupted.

"Please allow me to…"

"No, no, please don't trouble yourself, we know the way and will let ourselves out. Miss Winifred, if you please." Winnie bowed her head gracefully, as during this meeting she had conducted herself remarkably well. And was most definitely more behaved than what I had personally been granted an insight to. But I liked that most of all, as if I was the only one that would ever see this mischievous side of her. In truth, it made me feel special and singled out.

And just like when I had first greeted her, she whispered her goodbyes to me now in the most seductive voice,

"Good day Ad… Mr Fitzwilliam." Then when no one

was looking she winked at me again. Just as she had done when entering and captivating me once more with her beauty. She wore a handsome mint green dress that was corseted at the back and was held tight to her body. Doing so in such an enticing way that I wished to tug at the ties to the gift I wanted to unwrap.

Elbow-length cuffed sleeves lay sweetly over a chemise I wanted to lift from her petite frame, before sliding off each of her long gloves, leaving nothing but the pearls at her ears and neck. I wanted to expose the full beauty of her deep red hair, curls of which had been teasing me during this whole time. For I longed to push them back from her face, to meet with the curls perfectly coiled over one shoulder.

I knew the moment my mother saw her that even she couldn't deny her extreme beauty, which no doubt only added to her disdain and distinct dislike for her. This before she even had chance to open her mouth. As for me, I was more focused on the colour of her dress and wondering if she had chosen it with me in mind after I had last told her my new favourite colour.

I heard the front door close, signalling that they had left, and I felt my shoulders tense because of it. In fact, my entire body was now coiled like a snake ready to pounce, for my mood had quickly turned sour enough to strike. This was not helped by the first thing my mother said,

"Adam, you are not to see Miss Ambrogetti again, do I make myself clear?" I released a sigh before trying to explain the reasons why I would be choosing miss Winifred as a wife.

"But Mother…"

"No buts, Adam, it does not become you. The girl does not hold the adequate birthright and is not of high enough nobility for our family. No, you will marry Cousin Mary, as your late father and I discussed." My mother interrupted as she usually did, and I had the urge to argue. This after now discovering what had been my mother's plan all along. Cousin Mary. Good Lord, that would be like the equivalent of marrying a younger version of my mother! For she was younger than I, but behaved more like the old shrew that I was looking upon right now.

No, there was most definitely no way I was marrying Cousin Mary. However, I knew there was little point in saying this now, for it was clear I had to make a plan.

So, I decided to placate her and said in the tone of defeat, one I knew would fool her as it usually did in times like this,

"Yes, Mother."

STEPHANIE HUDSON

FIFTEEN

MISSING MISS WINNIE

2ND NOVEMBER 1680

Good Heavens, I missed her.

I was loath to say, but the next time I was to see my Winnie was weeks later, for unexpectedly, that same business that had taken me away for three days, had now mysteriously come about that I should be away for a few weeks. I had a feeling my mother was behind this, seeing as the man who owned the law firm I worked for was a good friend of hers. Therefore, my case was switched, and I was whisked off to Shrewsbury.

Of course, I also had a feeling this was because this so

happened to be where Cousin Mary lived, and was someone I was unfortunately forced to see. However, I made these rare occasions brief and to the point. In fact, there were only a few words more than what could be classed as being rude actually exchanged. In this time, I had least been able to communicate with Winnie, first when sending her a letter apologising for my abrupt departure, telling her that I was loathe to leave and I would count the days until I was back.

I also gave her a forwarding address for if she wished to write to me, making it well known how much this would please me. What I hadn't fully expected was just how much it would please me, for I didn't receive just one letter, I received fourteen of them. All of which arrived the same day and were labelled with the names of the days of the week. The first letter was labelled to be read on my first day and so on. For her first gave me clear instructions that I was to open each letter daily and not before.

I had to say, in truth, it was hard to restrain myself from tearing them all open and devouring every word she wrote. But this felt dishonest and as if I would be the cause of spoiling some game of hers. So, I refrained and by the end, I was glad of it, for it had offered me such a delightful reprieve from arduous working days, whereas I would just find myself questioning what she was doing in that same moment as I.

In her letters she was as delightful as she was in person, for it felt like just the two of us. She did not hold back in her feelings, and I would often find myself rather being touched by her words and her honesty, or laughing aloud at some quick anecdote or story she had to tell. She told me that she had gone back to get some more hot chocolate, but she felt so forlorn at not having me there with her, that it affected the taste, and she did not care for it without me.

I swear, after reading that upon waking, I continued the rest of my day with a ridiculous smile permanently etched on my face. But no matter how sweet her words were or how funny, they did not make up for the lack of her presence.

I missed her terribly, and had I not been relying that on keeping my job as a solicitor it would be a good enough income for us, then I would have promptly left my lodgings and gone back to her. But alas, I knew the importance of keeping my job, for I had a feeling that when I announced to my mother that I was intent on marrying Miss Winifred, then I would no doubt be cast out without an inheritance.

I was delighted to discover that as soon as I was back, I had a letter waiting for me, for I knew she could not welcome me home in person, but she wanted her words to be the first to greet me anyway. Again, I was touched by her thoughtfulness. She also hinted at where she might be and as soon as I had stepped through the door and read her letter, I found myself stepping right back out again. In fact, in my haste in looking for her I found myself bumping straight into the very being I had been searching for.

Instantly, my arms extended around her to prevent her from falling and in turn, she placed her hands against my chest as I pulled her closer. Both of our breaths held as if caught there and seized like prisoners for fear that this moment would end. But unfortunately, end it would, for once more we found ourselves out in the open and not with the privacy I craved when with her. Again, she was without an escort, and had this not been to my advantage, I would have found myself more annoyed at the chance of something happening to her. As it was, my mind could not linger on this for long, giving way to something more important, like greeting her.

"Miss Winifred, I beg of your forgiveness, I was not looking where I was headed and therefore the fault is mine."

"Mr Fitzwilliam, you are far too hard upon yourself, I fear my mind was elsewhere also and I find it strange that it walked me straight into the path of the root of those thoughts," she said, making my heart beat harder within my chest, for her easy admittance had both shocked me and enthralled me.

"You were thinking of me, my Lady?" I asked, wishing to hear of it again and this time her answer could not be denied, for she was making her feelings very clear.

"*Always,*" she whispered softly.

My own reaction to this was to gasp, for it was as I had been hoping for. In fact, I found myself so shocked I could do little but just stare down at her, captivated by those eyes of hers beseeching me. In the end she squirmed underneath my gaze, and I had to question if she knew of the carnal thoughts that heated them and spoke of what I wanted to do to her.

"Will you take a turn with me, Mr Fitzwilliam?" I looked around, hoping that there was somewhere more secluded so I could declare my own feelings to her in return. Unfortunately, there was not.

"It would be my pleasure, Miss Winifred," I said, and

instead of pulling her up against me once more and igniting those breathy responses from her, I offered her my arm like a gentleman.

"Do you come to Green Park often, and without an escort, I might add?" I asked letting my annoyance be known that she was again without an escort, but her response surprised me yet again, for she giggled.

"Are you worried about me, Sir?" she enquired with a mischievous eye. I didn't delay in my response.

"Yes. I think your uncle should be more careful with your safety."

"Have no fear, dear Fitzwilliam, I have a loyal foot servant who keeps watch over me but has the good sense to know when he is really needed." Hearing this surprised me for I had never seen this person, which prompted me to have a look around now to see if there was anyone watching us from afar. I felt a slight squeeze of her fingers at my arm, prompting me to look down at her. Upon doing so, I found that sweet smile and pretty face gazing up at me. It was then that I decided to give up my search and believe in her words.

"Very good then." I decided as we walked to make conversation, and for some reason I did so this time feeling somewhat more nervous.

"Did you know it was Charles II, who made the bulk of this land into the Royal Park it is known as today, being that of upper St James's Park. He had it designed, laying out the park's main walks and he even had built an icehouse here to supply him with ice for cooling drinks in summer. Have you seen it?" I asked, allowing my gaze to shamefully wonder, as it was not to be helped. Not with how she looked in that beautiful dress, one that accentuated her luscious curves to the point that it became a mission to keep my eyes from travelling to them.

"An ice house? I can imagine, given this weather, it to be full indeed." I laughed at her little joke, for it was unusually cold this time of year and not far away from granting us the snow. I was about to enquire to whether or not she was cold, for the cloak she wore around her shoulders did not seem adequate enough for my liking. I decided instead of expressing as much, to ensure another meeting between us, which was why I asked her,

"Tell me, do you enjoy the playhouse?"

"I do, Sir," she said, giving me a questioning look and one that was curious, for I felt something deeper was hidden there.

"Have you yet seen Nathaniel Lee's Theodosius at Dorset Garden?" I asked, knowing that if I was to take her to see a play, it would be as far away from Drury Lane as I could get.

"I can't say I have but I would very much like to." I smiled down in response, happy in the knowledge that I would be seeing her again.

"I thought you might, given the origins of the play," I teased, expecting her to ask me my meaning when she surprised me.

"Given by God," she said, tapping her finger against her lip as if deep in thought.

"My Lady?" I enquired, pulling back slightly so we would stop, and this time we both turned as if of the same mind, needing to look at each other fully.

"Yes, it is quite fitting, don't you think?" she answered quizzically, and I raised a brow at her in question before voicing my confusion.

"I am afraid I do not follow, my Lady."

"Theodosius, it is Greek, and it means 'Given by God', which makes it a perfect play to watch together as our time is given by the Gods, is it not?" she said, utterly astounding me and it reminded me of the cryptic answer she gave about the Gods weeks ago. It made me feel as if our meeting each other was somewhat fated, and I had to confess... *I liked the idea greatly.*

"Perfectly put, my dear," I said, unable to stop myself from lifting her hand to my mouth and kissing the back of it without taking my eyes from her. Doing so in hopes that it would say more than my lips were currently at liberty to speak. We continued to walk for a little bit further before Winifred's next question had me smirking for a different reason.

"Pray tell me, does Mrs Fitzwilliam like the theatre?" I had to refrain from laughing aloud and instead answered her question with a knowing look, for she was cunning in her response.

"No, my mother does not approve and therefore is never seen at the playhouse." Her look in return was a classic one I was starting to become accustomed to, and it was one that had me laughing aloud, unable to help myself this time.

This was after she said with a grin...

"Perfect."

STEPHANIE HUDSON

SIXTEEN

AN UNKNOWN TRAGEDY
5TH NOVEMBER 1680

"Winifred, what are we doing here?" I enquired, the moment I found myself standing outside a place I vowed never to go again.

"Oh, I know that you said about seeing Nathaniel Lee's Theodosius at Dorset Garden, but I thought as there was a new play opening tonight, we should be among the first to discover it together," she said and for the first time...

It wasn't what I wanted to hear.

"What is this play?" I asked forcing the words out, for my mind was far too preoccupied and otherwise engaged on the lingering hope that I was not going to bump into a certain someone whilst here with my Winnie.

"It is by Thomas Otway and called the Orphan, and I must confess, I was intrigued given the circumstances of my own situation." The moment she said this, what I knew was my once tense gaze softened, before I patted her hand that was in the crook of my arm. Because now was not the time to give way to my own turbulent thoughts. No, now was the time in offering her comfort, as I now understood better her reasons for bringing me here and even though I did not relish in the idea of ever stepping foot back into this place, I did so now with Winifred by my side, and *this gave me strength.*

I paid for my usual box, handing over the eight shillings, knowing at the very least I would be alone with her in the dark. As I very much doubted with this being so, that I would be concentrating at all on what was happening on the stage. Not when I would be free to gaze upon her for a whole evening uninterrupted, and with no one around to lay witness to it but her. And in truth, I liked the idea of being able to make her squirm under my heated gaze, letting her know without words just what it was she did to me.

We walked through the lobby, and I removed my hat, momentarily glancing down at myself to see that my state of dress was still in order. I had to say her reaction upon seeing me tonight was one I would not forget. For, in truth, it felt as though I was being undressed by her eyes alone, and once again, it was I that was found blushing. My long red coat was one of my finest, with its golden thread creating an artistic frame around the gold buttons that lined the jacket. This theme continued with a long waistcoat underneath, matching that of what was above it. The wide rimmed cuffs were as always folded back to reveal black satin, where the lace of my shirt could be seen underneath. I combined this with black stockings, black heeled shoes, and with the sight of lace, ruffled at my neck. I also had in my possession a walking stick, for this served its purpose for there was a blade hidden inside and had been a gift from my father.

But whatever my image may be in her eyes, it was nothing compared to what her own image did to me, for my eyes lingered far longer. Her dress was, as always, a beautiful one. One I had not yet seen before. In fact, I had not seen her in the same outfit twice, telling me that her uncle was at the very least keeping her well stocked in

London's latest fashions. Her dress was another vibrant green, and this time with a panelled front that had swirls of gold on both the bodice and underskirt. As for the top layer, a green silk that matched her eyes perfectly, finished at the elbow and was decorated with layers of lace reaching her forearms. A dark cloak wrapped around her shoulders, and I knew it was no doubt one she would be keeping on during the performance, due to the amphitheatre style of the Theatre Royal.

As for her hair, it was once again perfectly coiled in an attractive style on the top of her head, creating a cascade of curls to escape the back. A peacock feathered clasp enriched with pearls was the adornment for such a style and lay delicately over her hair. A simple string of pearls graced her neck, and these I had seen before, causing the same carnal thoughts to come to mind when seeing them, as how I wished I could bare her naked to me, wearing nothing but those pearls. I would gaze down upon them before seeing the beauty in her eyes as I made love to her, over and over again.

The sound of her voice brought me out of my lustful thoughts as we navigated our way through the crowd.

"Now, I am not one to usually give merit to idle

gossip, but in this case, I heard that the writer of this play, Thomas Otway, had written this particular play after being inspired by his own *unrequited love*," she said, comically whispering this last part in an overly dramatic fashion. I smiled down at her.

"That is sad indeed for any love that is not returned... is... *is a painful one*," I said with a strained tone, knowing that there were no better fitting words better to be said in this place. Although, now I continued to question if that was love at all, for I had not felt one hundredth of what I did for Miss Winnie.

"Your response... it is, well... almost like you were speaking from experience," Winifred said, making me wince, as I should have known for there was very little that she did not pick up on. Thankfully, though I did not have to answer, for the crowd ushered us forward and I had to hold on to her arm, so we did not get separated in the mass.

In 1672, only eight years ago, the theatre had caught fire and the owner, Thomas Killigrew built a larger theatre on the same plot. This was renamed as the 'Theatre Royal in Drury Lane' which reopened two years after in 1674. This information I had learned from Margaret, who was often asked to star in the play's cast, for she was a private friend of Thomas Killigrew. This now made me wonder if she was, in fact, more than just friends. It seemed likely so.

The Theatre Royal was more of an amphitheatre in its style of building, being that it was open air over what was known as the pit. This was where the less expensive tickets were bought, for these were filled with benches without backs and covered in green cloth. It was also where most of the giddy chatter was to be found.

Rows of box seats as they were known, surrounded the walls of the theatre, and were reserved for a higher class, given that they provided a better view. However, the private box I had obtained was one I paid extra for, so I would be assured of the privacy. I just hoped as we made our way towards it, that Winifred missed the head nods of acknowledgement that were sent my way. This was mainly by the theatre staff who were used to seeing me here on a regular occurrence not so long ago. In truth, I had been so blind I had spent most of my evenings here in hopes of being granted a few spare minutes alone with Margaret at the end of each performance.

What had surprised me though was her very last performance I'd seen. This was one unlike any other before it, for the crowd had been unusually silent, and at the end of her last song, there had been barely even a single applause in the audience, for it was as if everyone had been rendered mute. In fact, she had run off the stage in tears and at the time I had felt nothing but empathy for her. I had hoped that she would find solace and comfort in my arms, not realising that it would be found in the arms of another man. Arms that would offer something far more, and no doubt, for far less a cost.

As for the stage, it was set up now for an entirely different production and from up here you could see the grooves in the wood. These were used for the wings and flats to be moved, in addition to trapdoors in the floor. I knew this theatre inside and out, and therefore I knew that the proscenium arch was used to cover the stage equipment above, that even included a pair of girondels. These were large wheels holding many a candle, which was used as a way to counteract the light from the footlights.

"Fitzwilliam, are you alright, you seem rather quiet?" Winifred asked in a concerned tone, and as we took our seats, I patted her hand and told her,

"All is well." I would have said more but it was clear the play was starting, and I was soon to learn it was a tragedy about love. Acasto, a nobleman, retired from court and was now living in the country, encourages his sons Castalio and Polydore to stay home and concentrate on their studies. But, more importantly, to avoid the company of women.

"A protective father indeed, I do wonder if there will ever be any mother found, one so protective as to ward her sons away from that of her own sex… for I believe Acasto thinks of woman as being dangerous creatures and not to be trusted… what are your thoughts on this?" Winifred whispered this question to me with a knowing glint in her eye, tugging down at my jacket as if needing the excuse to touch me. Not that she ever did, for I would always welcome such affection. But her playful question made me smirk down at her. It was clear in that moment she was most definitely in the know of my mother's interference, but then again, my mother wasn't exactly known for her subtlety.

"I believe he is somewhat right in his observations but then, I also think he is wrong in one important factor…" I whispered down at her in return, making her lean closer to me so she may whisper back enquiring my meaning.

"And what important factor may that be?" This was when I decided to give her a glimpse into the power she

held over me.

"It is only the right woman that is dangerous, the woman who claims a man's heart is the only one that holds the power of crushing it, and no other." Her response to this was a curious one and was not what I expected, for it seemed as if she had mistaken my meaning completely. She cast her eyes from the stage and looked down at her lap in a forlorn way.

"My Winnie?" I said, questioning if she was well and using my pet name for her in hopes of making her smile once more. But this was when she answered in a cryptic way, as if she had known my past without me even needing to speak of it.

"But perhaps it is another woman that then has the power to mend it... for surely if a woman has the power of making a man fall in love with her, then it stands to reason she also has the same power to heal such broken sentiments caused by another." Her words affected me so, for they could not have been more perfect, and it almost felt symbolic considering where we were. Which is why I took her hand in mine, and kissed the back of it, telling her,

"I could not have put it better myself for I agree with you entirely." Thankfully, my answer seemed like the right

one, for I was rewarded with that beaming smile of hers, before she cast her eyes back to the stage. However, my own gaze could not be so easily swayed away from her. This is not to say that I did not grasp some concept of what was happening within the play, for I knew Winifred was captivated by it and I in turn was captivated by her. But knowing what I knew of her, I thought it best to keep my wits about me and try to follow the storyline, for she would no doubt question me on it later. Questions I wanted to be prepared for as she would most definitely have her thoughts and no doubt offer them freely to me.

So, as the play continued, it introduced that of Acasto's ward, a young girl named Monimia. This made me wonder of her uncle's own guardianship over her and how he would feel about discovering my intentions towards his niece. I had the feeling that he would welcome the match, for he had certainly been forthcoming in allowing us to spend time together, and Winifred had often assured me over her uncle's liking to me.

"I wonder which one she will choose?" Winifred asked on a whisper as if she couldn't help herself, for she was getting totally immersed in the play. Of course she was referring to the twin sons Castalio and Polydore, both who

considered themselves to be in love with Monimia. They both vied for the claim to woo her first, but one brother was more deceitful than the other, for he secretly contracted himself to marrying her, however Polydore overheard this and made plans to replace Castalio on the wedding night.

"Oh, I can see where this is going, pesky twin... classic." Winifred commented cryptically as if she was not surprised by this certain turn of events. But then again, she had picked this play for a reason, having already heard about it. I found myself wondering whether she had been recommended it by a friend, for she rarely spoke about anyone other than her uncle. Actually, I found this rather odd and the more I thought about it, the stranger it seemed.

"Three soft strokes on the chamber door, how exciting," she commented again, as it was at a part in the play where the switch had been made by using the wedding-night signal.

"I don't see this ending well, do you?" Winifred whispered, and again I had to bite my bottom lip from laughing as she seemed to be constantly talking throughout the whole play, asking me questions. Whereas most would probably find this annoying, I found it incredibly endearing.

"I believe you are right, for there is tragedy in the air,"

I teased her back, making her quietly giggle. Of course, I was not wrong, for in the play it was soon discovered the next day what had happened, now with only the prospect of death for those involved to be expected. For in the end, Polydore provoked his brother Castalio into a duel and ran into his brother's sword on purpose, making Winnie cover her mouth and gasp like others in the audience. After this, Monimia takes a fatal draught of poison and Castalio stabs himself, thus concluding the tragedy. Everyone rose from their seats and applauded the actors for their impressive portrayal of characters played. Meanwhile, I couldn't help but reach out and tap my little Winnie under the chin for she now looked utterly forlorn.

"Hey, come now... what is that sad face for?" I questioned, and then she looked up at me with those big green and blue eyes of hers, and said,

"I don't understand, I see very little reason why everyone had to die." At this I couldn't help it, but I laughed, making her quickly frown back up at me. I bit my lip to stop and said with mirth in my eyes,

"Forgive me, dearest."

"Why do you laugh, it is sad, is it not?" she questioned, and again it only had me laughing, and even harder this time as we walked out of the box. I swear I could barely contain it, and she grinned up at me before nudging me with her elbow. I couldn't help it, but I pulled her in closer to me and whispered down at her,

"Sweetheart, you brought me to see a tragedy, what did you expect would happen?" At this she smirked, giving me a beaming smile, before telling me in that sweet soft tone of hers,

"I thought love would conquer all."

"Oh, my Winnie…" I whispered, just as I was lowering my head, for now was the time I had to seal such sweetness with a kiss. A kiss I would have finally taken had it not been for the sound of my name being called, and one I utterly loathed to hear coming from such a woman.

"Fitzwilliam, I thought it was you," Margaret said now coming up to me, before giving a distasteful look at Winnie.

"You! What are you doing here?!" Margaret asked in a distasteful tone, making me frown and stand a little further in front of Winnie in a protective manner, for I did not care for the way she spoke to her.

"That is enough, Margaret, you will not speak to my…" I paused, biting my own damn tongue before saying the word fiancé, for it had not been how I had wanted to announce such. I hadn't even asked the girl yet, nor the permission of her uncle. But damn it to Hell if I did not want to make the claim now!

"Your what? For it was not long ago that you were found knocking on my door!" she snapped, and I was now questioning why I ever found such a being worthy of my time, let alone my affections. But then it was in this moment that Winifred had had enough and decided to take matters into her own hands. She stepped back to my side and placed her hand around my stomach in an intimate embrace. She was definitely making her intentions known in the claim and my heart swelled because of it.

"Yes, well now he is knocking on my door, and let it be known that when I open it, I do not have another lover hidden inside!" she snapped, shocking me and now quickly having me questioning what exactly it was that Winnie knew, and more importantly... *how?*

Margaret huffed at this, and snapped,

"You are welcome to him!" Winnie gripped me to her in a tighter hold and replied,

"But of course I am, for your loss is my gain, now if you will excuse us, we have somewhere important to be, don't we, dearest?" After this was said and her point had been eloquently made, she looked up at me as if I was the only man in the world. I nodded once and put an arm around her slight shoulders, tucking her into my side as we made our way past a now flustered Margaret.

It now had to be said, that as much as I had dreaded the encounter, I found that Margaret had nothing to do with why my mind was now in turmoil. No, now it was full of questions. Questions I was intent on getting the answers to as I led her from the theatre, I let it also be known where my thoughts were headed, for once we were outside, Winnie spotted her own carriage, and was walking towards it when I grabbed her hand. I pulled her back to me with such force she fell into me, and I wrapped my arms around her.

"Fitzwilliam?" she questioned in an uncertain tone, which was when I told her,

"We have a lot to discuss you and I." I watched as she notably swallowed hard before those damn eyes of hers drew me in like a foolish moth to the flame. For the spell she was weaving over my heart was one that could not be denied. Which was why I let loose the beast of a man inside of me and growled down at her...

"And it's Adam to you."

SEVENTEEN

REASON FOR MISTRUST
5TH NOVEMBER 1680
WINIFRED

It was in this moment I knew I had gone too far. Lucius had warned me not to go down this path and he had been right. But then I had to be sure. I had to be sure that his affections for me were not founded solely from just having his heart broken, and I had not just been left with the pieces whilst she had still been left with the core. I had not expected to run into her, but I thought it enough to see if there was any need for my concerns by gauging his actions just by simply being there.

I had wanted to know if he would converse in conversation as easily as he had done with me many times before. I wanted to know if his gaze would wander from the sight of me, which it rarely did when we were together. But had he been looking for her, then I knew he would not be looking at me.

Thankfully, however, none of this had happened and he seemed as content with me as he usually did. So, we left the box with me believing in the blissful notion that he had once and for all forgotten the name of Margaret. That, of course, was until the very essence of that loathsome name had showed up and reminded him.

He looked utterly appalled, and the way he had tried to protect me against her tone, one he obviously did not care to be cast my way, made my heart flutter. These past weeks had been some of the best in my entire life, and I had merely fallen harder and deeper and more fervent than I ever could have imagined. There had been many a time I wanted to throw myself at him, to drag him to some dark corner somewhere and have my wicked way with him. But then I knew, as a mortal gentleman, one that had been raised by good morals no doubt… *although, truth be known, this was questionable after visiting his mother…* I still knew I had to take things slow.

For I did not want him to think ill of me. I didn't want him to think that I acted this brazen way with every man that I met. I didn't want him to compare me to… *her.* I needed him to understand what he meant to me, and to do that in today's world meant hinting at it, before coming right out and just saying it.

Of course, there had been moments that I hadn't been able to help myself in making it quite clear that I was bestowing my affections upon him for a reason. But again, he remained the perfect gentleman. And he wished me to call him Adam. However, right now when it was growled down to me like that, it did grant me cause to worry. I had never seen him angry or upset and being cast down upon me, only on Margaret.

But then I knew where my mistakes lay, and these were solely at my own feet. For it was now abundantly clear that I knew about Adam long before he knew about me. I didn't want to lie to him but how was I to tell him a truth without first backing it up with a lie, for until he turned into one of the supernatural and took possession of Abaddon, then he could know none of my world. Therefore, I was forced to lie about it all.

"Winifred, this is when you start talking, for do not tell me that you have run out of speech now," he said, looking down at me and slowly walking me backwards towards the carriage and out of earshot of other theatregoers that were done for the night.

"I... I..." I couldn't find the words, and I looked down at the cobbled street and mumbled,

"I'm sorry."

"You're sorry... good heavens, woman, what could you be sorry for... do not tell me that your affections were as deceitful as hers, by God do not tell me that I have fallen fool to the same folly once more... not by you, by anyone but you! For my heart would definitely not take such a blow!" he said with such emotion that my heart broke, and I raised up my hand and cupped his cheek telling him,

"Please, please, Adam, don't ever think that, don't ever mistrust how I feel for you. I am nothing like her... nothing... I implore you, Adam, please... please do not cast me and her under the same harsh light. I'm nothing like that woman, for she barely even deserves the claim!" I said, and he closed his eyes before looking off to one side as if trying to understand.

"Then make me understand, Winifred. Explain to me

how it is you knew her and me… you knew of our past acquaintance before I had ever laid eyes on you? Was the carriage real or was that just a plot to get to me?"

"No!" he raised a brow at my answer, and I realised my mistake.

"I mean yes… I mean, Gods, I don't know what I mean!" I explained, and his eyebrows shot up as he snapped,

"Gods? I am intrigued for how many do you have, for I doubt any of them right now would aid you in covering up your deceit!" Hearing this was like receiving ten lashes to my heart, as I was soon discovering I had a fatal weakness.

"Please don't shout at me, I can't bear it when you shout at me," I said in a small voice, making him wince before releasing a sigh. Then he gripped me tighter and whilst looking down at me he said,

"Please, just answer me one thing."

"Anything," I whispered, for it was true, I would have given this man anything he asked of me.

"Please tell me it was real, please tell me that what I felt for you was real and what you felt in return was not just to lead me on a fool's errand." The desperation in his voice was felt at the very centre of my soul.

"Oh, Adam… yes, it was real, all of it… every moment since I met you. I… I feel as if I need to explain…" I said, breaking away from a sentence that would have ended in me confessing my love for him and after now being caught in what was my own innocent deceit, I feared now was not the time.

"Allow me, my dear." Lucius' voice seemed to come from nowhere, when in fact it had most likely come from my carriage.

"Uncle?" I said, keeping up the ruse.

"My servant was detained so I decided to come in person to escort you back home, only I fear I have walked in on an unfortunate discussion. I apologise, I do not wish for you to believe that I was listening, but it was hard not to hear from the open window of the carriage."

"It's alright, Uncle," I said in a quiet tone.

As for Adam, he didn't look as if he wanted to let me go anytime soon and what it took for him to do so was when Lucius cleared his throat. Then he reminded him of this fact, by telling him,

"If you would be so kind as to release my niece, Fitzwilliam, for I fear you are scaring her." At this, Adam instantly let me go, now looking at his hands as if questioning why they had been gripping on to me so tightly in the first place.

"Forgive me, but I fear it would be best to interject at this point and if you would be so kind as to allow me to explain, whereas my niece is struggling," Lucius said, making Adam grant him a curt nod of his head before answering,

"Go ahead."

"I fear you and I have been folly to the same despicable woman and were led to believe that our affections meant more than the weight of our purses. We were under the same misconception that our affections were given in return." At this my mouth dropped open and when Adam wasn't looking, Lucius nudged me and tapped himself under the chin, telling me to close my mouth before I was caught.

"You... *and Margaret?*" he asked, clearly shocked.

"Alas, I am ashamed to say it, but it is true."

"And what does this have to do with Winifred?" Adam asked, crossing his arms over his chest and looking bigger for it.

"I made the mistake of taking my niece to see her last show, something Margaret did not believe I was capable of attending. I wished to surprise her, and I wanted to introduce her to my niece for I had not done so before. I foolishly believed that this was the next step to take in securing her affections and taking our relationship potentially further," Lucius said, making this story incredibly believable as I was already half believing it myself and I knew it wasn't true! Perhaps Lucius could make a good career out of being a playwright himself, he certainly had the talent for it.

"I think I can see where this is going, but continue," Adam said with his jaw tense.

"Like you, I intended on meeting her backstage, and was to knock on her dressing room door, but I am ashamed to say, I was then forced to witness that I was not the first there to knock. Nor would I have been the second it seems, for that claim is your own." I watched as Adam swallowed a hard lump before looking at me and seeing my solemn face. One he thought was no doubt out of pity for his unfortunate situation. But, in fact, it was nothing more than being riddled with guilt due to being forced now to stand here and allow Lucius' lies to continue.

"And Winifred... she was with you and saw all of this?" he asked as if the idea of this horrified him.

"That she did, and I am ashamed that she was to learn

of a young woman's deceit in this way. I had hoped to shield her from such things, being that she is such a sweet-tempered girl herself, I wanted to keep her innocent of such debauchery." At this I couldn't help but cough to stop myself from reacting in another way, as innocence wasn't usually a word I would hear when describing my nature... naughty and mischievous, most certainly. On occasion, well I had once been a damn good thief. Hell, and as for debauchery, that could have been my middle name!

"However, Winifred was so angry on your behalf that it wasn't long after you left, that she stormed right up to Margaret and had a few stern words for her," Lucius said, finishing his story and thus giving cause to all that just happened in the theatre.

"On behalf of yourself, no doubt," Adam added.

"Yes, well, my niece knows that I have a stronger constitution when it comes to fickle woman... although, I confess, if you hadn't hit the man, then I most certainly would have... had my niece not been there of course... so for that, I thank you." Adam's lips quirked at this before the next big question arose.

"And the carriage?" I flinched at this, wondering how he was going to save me from this one, as it seemed a bit implausible to me for such a coincidence to happen, for London was a big place indeed.

"Yes, well, that was an unfortunate event, but I will confess, Winifred had felt so strongly towards you after hearing your name, she inquired after you and discovered your address," Lucius said, without even needing to take a moment and therefore making it very convincing.

"I did? I mean I... I did, that's right," I said, turning what was a questioning tone into a knowing one and hopefully quick enough for Adam not to question it. Lucius shot me a look to say oh so many things that he could not in front of Adam, and foolish no doubt only being one of them.

"She was on her way there to call upon you and see if you were well after the night's events, when I caught up with her and asked her not to be so hasty. I fear her silence was on my account for I did not want my dealings with Margaret to be discussed between anyone. I was ashamed and Winifred, being of a good sort, was kind enough to keep my secret for me," Lucius told him, and if I was honest, in my eyes he was hitting Shakespeare status.

"That is understandable, for I too have kept such knowledge from being heard," Adam admitted.

"Winifred, not wanting to be dishonest, therefore

decided to return and in doing so, got herself caught in the middle of the street about to be thrown down which could have ended in a disastrous outcome. But thanks to you, this did not happen after you gallantly stepped in and rescued her from such fate. Unfortunately, at that juncture, she did not feel comfortable exposing the truth in letting you know that she had already seen you once before," Lucius said, finishing this second part of our deceitful plan and twisting it so it became something Adam would easily believe, and I had to say it was a damn convincing one at that.

"I see," Adam said, now looking at me as I could feel his gaze, yet it was one I was not brave enough to challenge back with granting him my own.

"Very well, now that's all settled I will leave you two a moment alone to say your goodbyes. But, I will ask, Fitzwilliam, if you would be so kind as to keep my story between us, indeed I would be most grateful," Lucius said nodding to him.

"You have my word, Sir, as a gentleman, it will not go beyond the three of us, and I in turn, will ask you of the same on my own behalf." Lucius nodded before shaking his hand and turning to me, saying,

"I will wait in the carriage for you, dearest one." I

nodded and let him walk past me so that I could be alone with Adam. Yet in doing so, I now felt the weight of guilt lay heavily against me, for the lies that had been told were lies I was not proud of, no matter how good Lucius' story was. But it was my own fault as I should have just heeded his words and never come to this damn place.

I cleared my throat of emotion enough to tell him,

"I understand if this changes things between us." This was said not faking the hopeless tone of voice that came from me. I heard Adam release a deep sigh before whispering,

"Oh, Winnie." Then, before I could respond, he stepped up to me, taking hold of my chin and raising my face up so I could not deny him my eyes anymore. Then, once assured I would not look away, he graced the backs of his fingers down my cheek before running the pad of his thumb across my lips, making me close my eyes and release my own sigh this time.

"I fear I must let you go…" he said, making me cry out and grip on to his jacket as if I could prevent him from walking away.

"Oh no! Please, Adam, I…" At this he smiled and leant in closer to whisper in my ear.

"I do not mean that I am willing to let you go completely, I only mean for tonight… as tomorrow I will see you, for we will have much to discuss of the future. But until then, sleep well, my dear, sweet Winnie." Then he kissed my cheek, and stepped away, leaving me now so that I no other choice but to get into the carriage. I knew that, for the moment I stood there staring at him longingly only made him nod his head, telling me silently to get into the carriage. So, I did and by the time I looked around, Adam was nowhere to be seen.

"I hope this doesn't mean that he's going back in there to face her, for I fear that means that our story will quickly unravel," I said to Lucius, who strangely had started grinning at me.

"And if you have any desire to tell me I told you so, then you can think better of it." At least he shrugged his shoulders and then responded,

"Around you, I have a feeling that I will have many a year ahead of me with which to be granted the opportunity to say it."

"Umpf." I made the sound and didn't respond further, instead looking longingly back into the distance of where we had come from.

"He still does not trust us, and I believe he now needs reassurances as to what we said was true," Lucius commented but strangely looked unaffected by this, despite all that was relying on this plan to work.

"Then you think he has gone back in there to confront her...? Oh Gods, we're screwed!" I shouted throwing up my arms.

"Screwed? Is this another word of yours that represents being fucked?" he asked with a smirk.

"Yes, that's pretty much the truth of it."

"Have no fear, little darling." I frowned at this and snapped,

"How can you say that...? I could see it in his eyes, Lucius, he was planning something... I swear if that woman makes one move towards him, Lucius, I will chop off her head, and mount it on the spikes of the Tower of London!"

"That is quite cutthroat for a little innocent lady under my guardianship," he commented ironically.

"You're a vampire, Lucius, I think it's quite fitting," was my retort, one he laughed at.

"Yes, well, your lover boy does not yet know that and for the meantime, let's try and keep it that way by refraining from the spilling of mortal blood… should we?" Alright, so this was admittedly good advice.

"Fine, I may not kill her, but I know far worse things that could befall her, and I would only be in need of a witch to cause her problems…"

"Like?" he enquired, making me tell him,

"Vaginal warts are not fun." At this, Lucius made a face of disgust down at my lady parts and I rolled my eyes.

"I didn't mean on me! Jeez, I am just saying that girls talk, you know, so I hear things," I said in my defence.

"Things I most likely don't want to know, so let's keep it that way as I enjoy fucking, immensely so, and therefore do not want any mental image to tarnish it," Lucius replied, making me laugh before telling him,

"Yes, well I think you're safe, Lucius, as you don't often hear of the supernatural being very susceptible to vaginal warts, or mouldy cocks and all manner of other body parts that can rot and fall off… so I think you're still safe sticking your cock in the supernatural."

"Well then, let that be the good news of the night," he said, making me grant him a wry look, and one he winked at.

"So, what are we going to do if he has gone back in

there and why do you seem so sure that he hasn't?" I asked, after a moment had passed. He laughed once before telling me,

"Because, little Imp…" he paused and grinned, leaning forward closer to me, at the same time moving back the curtain of the carriage door. Then he beckoned me closer with a jerk of his fingers. So, I looked, only to find another carriage behind us.

That's when he finished his sentence and told me…

"He's currently following us."

EIGHTEEN

PERFECTION UNDER THE MOONLIGHT
5ᵀᴴ NOVEMBER 1680
ADAM

I didn't know what compelled me to follow them, but I felt after tonight, I had lost some trust in Winifred. Of course, her uncle had been very convincing in his story and knowing now what I knew of Margaret's true intentions, it made it more than plausible. And well, no doubt verging on the highly probable. However, I had watched Winifred's face, and the shock I had seen there as her uncle's story had unfolded had not been what one would expect to see. For her look hadn't been one out of surprise that her uncle had chosen to be so forthcoming in his tale. No, it had seemed to be one born more from shock at the story itself. As if I was not alone in hearing this for the first time.

Of course, it was true that my cause for mistrust could now be solely based on experiencing Margaret's deceitfulness not long ago. But then, I also knew I would be a fool not to be cautious, for these past events had given me enough reason to doubt. But, the main reason for following them now, was that I had never been to their home. I had never seen their house and I had to be sure that in fact, they were not playing me, just as Margaret had done.

Now it was true that they may appear wealthy, but fine clothes could be bought by anyone. Perhaps this was some nefarious ruse of theirs. Her uncle didn't exactly seem old enough to hold the claim and it made me wonder if the two weren't in fact lovers. A couple praying on the wealthy with a pretty face and a 'woe is me' tale of being an orphan. A story that could have been one many had fallen prey to before me.

Of course, I utterly loathed to think like this. To think so badly of her actually caused me physical pain in my chest and had me rubbing a hand in the area as if this would ease my suffering. Because, in all honesty, I'd fallen in love with the girl. And foolishly to the point that I could look beyond most of her past transgressions and wrong doings. However, what I could not look past, is if she was in fact in love with another man. If she were currently spending her nights in another man's bed and he was not her uncle at all, but in fact her lover.

Even the name Lucius Septimus was a curious one and enough to grant cause to wonder itself. It was one I had never heard before, despite her claiming his foreign ancestry. No, I needed to be sure, and the only way to do that was to follow them now. Hoping, in my endeavour, not to find some cheap lodgings and in fact the grand Manor house that she had claimed he lived in was nothing more than another lie. But this was not all that troubled me and gave me cause for concern.

Because ever since I'd heard the story Lucius had told, I had one question left, burning a hole in my mind. Because, if what her uncle had stated to be the truth, then it made me question why she would ever think to pick this theatre?

And with her knowing of the pain that it would cause me, or worse still, knowing the chance of meeting

Margaret would force her uncle's secret out. Why would she be so reckless, so bold? It didn't make sense and I was determined to get answers, even if I had to prevail upon them at night, I didn't care, for I would not rest until I was satisfied.

I continued to follow the carriage ahead until we travelled towards East London, and to a place I didn't know well enough to make a full assessment. All I knew was that it was quite some distance away from town and heading toward the country. But then again, the moment I pulled up outside a large country estate I understood why, for it seemed someone liked their solitude, and a country house was preferred over a town house in the centre of the city. It suddenly made sense why I had not yet been invited here, and all our meetings so far had been suggested to be in town. For it was clear that Winifred had been thoughtful enough to want to make things easier for me.

At least that is what I hoped.

As for their carriage, it had already had its occupants disembark and had disappeared, no doubt to the coach house somewhere on the grounds. Which was why, when getting out myself, I asked my servant,

"Do you know of this place?"

"Aye, Sir, I do. I have a sister who works at the inn close by. She told me of this place, this be Eastbury Manor, and one of the finest estates in this area, owned by a rich landowner not many people know about, has a funny name," he answered.

"Yes, indeed it is," I mused, more to myself, wondering now of the origins of such a name.

"Very well. Pull the carriage out of sight and wait until I'm finished, I have a feeling I may be some time," I told him, making him nod.

"Aye, very good, Sir." My man did as he was told, and I was now faced with the grand red brick building that only ever spoke of one thing… extreme wealth. Meaning, more importantly,

They hadn't lied.

I swear I nearly fell to my knees and wept out of relief, I was so overcome by the emotion.

The house was laid out in the typical Tudor style, and I knew without even setting foot in it, that it would be a H style plan with a square courtyard at its centre. The Manor stood two storeys high with an attic above and no doubt, a cellar below. But it was the red brick that told me of its expense, for this was not a cheap product to produce and only the wealthiest could afford to build a brick house. Especially back when this house would have been first constructed. Of course, back then, glass was also expensive, telling me that this had been handed down to the man who owned it now and from a wealthy family. Again, my fears had been unfounded. Yet, despite the obvious wealth of the house and that no longer being of concern to me, the most important question of all still remained…

Why that theatre?

I walked up to the front door and was just about to knock when it was opened by none other than its owner, Lucius Septimus, her uncle. Then, without even enquiring as to why I was here, he told me,

"I believe you will find Winifred in the walled garden at the back of the house, she enjoys the solitude the night offers, and the scent of the flowers that fill the air." I couldn't help but frown in question for not only was it clear that he allowed his niece out at this time of night, but it was even more odd that he would encourage me to go and find her, for me to be alone with her in the dark, for there was only a hint of the moon casting its light, and just barely enough to see the pathway in front of me. For it would easily be another week before it was full again and filling the night sky with more glow.

I was about to grant him a response but before that could happen, he closed the door, clearly signalling that this meeting was over. I had a feeling it was because he knew that I had followed them, and that in itself was an untrustworthy act. One that I hoped to see rectified, for I did not want him thinking ill of me, not when I still hadn't had the chance to asked him for his niece's hand in marriage.

But then pride be damned, I would near beg the man if that was what it would take for him to grant me my every desire by giving me his consent. As God was my witness, if he said no then I would be inclined to try and convince her to run away with me, because I could not foresee my life without her. But, before that began, I needed my answers.

I walked the perimeter of the property until getting to a brick archway that led to the garden he spoke of. For once I viewed it as her uncle had explained, it was true that night offered a sweet solitude that day did not, and as I breathed in a heavy breath, I too took in the scents of flowers that seemed stronger now. Stronger and I did not know why.

I knew then, from that moment on, that when I was to make Winifred my wife, I would create a place for her like this. A place we could both come and share the peaceful experience together. I would create a quaint little seating area for us to enjoy the night, planting flowers I knew she would like. A place we could stare up at the moon and the stars and silently enjoy each other's company.

Although, knowing what I knew of Winifred I doubt silence was going to play much of a part in it. For one of the things I loved about her the most was that she was a talkative sort. One that had an expressive manner I adored watching. In truth, she entertained me greatly, and I knew that it would not be possible to ever tire of her and her exuberant ways.

After accessing the garden it did not take me long to find her, seeing as the gold on her dress lit up as if guiding me straight to her. She had her back to me, leaning in closer sniffing a perfect rose that she held cupped in her hand. The sight was a captivating one, and not one I would soon forget. Therefore, as if being trapped in the same spell as she, I couldn't help my reaction as I slowly crept up behind her. My aim was not to frighten her so she would scream, but only startle her enough that it would give me cause to wrap my arms around her once more.

My plan worked, for without her knowing yet of my

presence I leant in and whispered in her ear,

"It is not nearly as lovely as you, nor does it smell so sweet."

"Fitzwilliam!" she said in surprise, taking a step back as I thought she would. And in doing so granted me the result of my objective as her body was now pressed against my own, where I curled my arms around her and held her tight. Then I told her in a fervent tone,

"Caught at last, my Winnie."

"Adam... what are you doing here?" She asked me the right question, and now it was my turn to do the same.

"I could not wait for tomorrow, for my heart beats with anticipation for what your answers may be to the questions I have for you." At this, she turned around and I loosened my hold on her to allow this. She nodded her head and then held out her arm, motioning towards a fallen tree trunk. One that had clearly been left there for the sole purpose of being somewhere to sit amongst a pretty patch of wilderness.

"Shall we sit?" she asked, and I nodded, causing her to be the one to take my hand this time. Then I let myself be led over towards it, through the pathway that backed onto a bit of open field, one filled with wild flowers.

"I love coming here at night, just me and nature and the stars to grace its beauty," she said in that musical voice of hers, looking up now at the sky and I could see that she was right, a blanket of stars graced this moment in time.

"It is you that graces the beauty with that of your own, for I am in awe of you." Even in the moonlight I could see her blush as she looked down at her lap and smiled.

"You do me a great honour by gifting me with such compliments, despite you being here out of mistrust," she said, being so bold as to call me out on the reasons I was here. I shouldn't have been surprised for I knew that she missed nothing.

"You are right, and I can only apologise. I just needed to know that it was all real before I…" I took pause, needing to find the right words to explain.

"Before you what, tell me, Adam, what did you come all of this way to say?" Her voice was sweet and alluring, as if she could entice the deepest darkest secrets out of anyone… *myself included.*

"I will tell you, but first I have another question I need answering."

"Very well," she said, placing her hands upon her lap as if ready.

"I need to know, Winnie, if what your uncle said tonight was true, then what would possess you to want to go back there? Surely such a thing would have been too much of a risk?" At this she released a sigh and told me,

"Some risks are worth taking to get to the truth, just like the reason you're here now."

"Explain that to me," I gently commanded of her.

"You needed to know the truth, despite what it could have done to our relationship, you came here to seek answers just like I took you back to the theatre to seek my own, for I too needed to be sure." This shocked me.

"Sure, of what, my affections for you?" I asked in astonishment, not believing for one moment I had given her any cause for doubt.

"To be sure that your affections were not still… *with her also,*" she admitted painfully, and I sucked in a quick breath. This, before I took up her hand in mine and started playing with her fingertips with the need to touch her being too much to deny. Then I asked her,

"You believed that I may still have affections for her, and that you were a mere distraction from the pain I suffered?" I admit when she nodded her head slightly, I knew I had been correct in my assumption.

"Oh, Winnie… and did you discover your answer, and was it also one worth the risk to gain, like you claim?" It was at this point she lifted her head up and finally looked at me.

"Yes, Adam, I got my answer, and it was most definitely worth it." At this, I closed my eyes and let her words wash over me. For it was clear now that there were no more barriers between us. We were letting our emotions free from the constraints the convention of society had set against us and in doing so, what some would no doubt deem as impropriety. But I didn't care! For there was no one here but God himself to lay witness. And I most certainly did not think that he would cast judgement on such declarations of love. For in my eyes, love was not a sin and nor should it ever be looked upon as so.

"Please, Winifred, do not trifle with my emotions, please just tell me… do you… *do you love me?*" I forced the words out, despite being terrified of the potential crushing outcome that such an answer could award me. But then, equally so, it could also award me the Heaven that I prayed her words would take me to. All I needed was a simple yes and I knew she would be mine forever.

It was at this point that she got up and the moment her

hand was about to slip from mine, I grasped it tighter and said a panicked,

"No, don't go, Winnie." This was when she smiled down at me, and then she cupped my cheek, before telling me,

"Oh, my love, I'm not going anywhere." Then, as I was still startled by her admission in calling me such a sweet endearment, my shock continued as she lifted up her skirts, so she could sit astride me in my lap. My hands instantly framed her waist, and my cock instantly rose to the occasion, despite this clearly not being her intention. No, her intention became clear the moment she framed each side of my face with her small hands.

Then she told me,

"Adam, I have loved you from the very first moment I saw you and I will continue to do so until the very last moment, one I hope never ever comes, for my one wish is to be granted an eternity with you." Then she leant down and finally, my world was complete...

As she kissed me.

NINETEEN

HEART TO HEART
10TH NOVEMBER 1680

I slammed the door on my way out, having little time for my mother's interference in my life, because after that glorious moment when Winifred kissed me, my mind and heart were set. For all I had needed to hear was how she loved me, and after that, I had lost my mind and my heart to her, for she had consumed both along with every other piece of me. She owned my soul, and I longed to tell her this combined with those same three words that I was still yet to say. I was so eager in fact, I was concerned that the next time I did see her I would just burst out saying them at the most impromptu moment, startling her with my admission.

I had intended to tell her how I felt, but of course, the moment she started kissing me everything else was lost and became shadowed under the perfection she gifted me. That most perfect moment under the moonlight and graced by God himself. It had been unlike anything I had ever experienced before. That kiss had meant everything to me, and I had never wanted it to end. Unfortunately, end it was forced to, because minutes later, her uncle cleared his throat and said,

"Come now, little dear, it is time that Fitzwilliam be getting home for I believe after tonight he has much to discuss with that of his family." At this, she beamed back at me and graced me with the biggest smile ever seen, before kissing me on my cheek and jumping from me. She was giddy in her behaviour and twirled her skirts around, telling me,

"Soon, my love. Until I see you soon, my handsome prince!" Then she skipped in a childlike manner to her uncle before pausing next to him and kissing him on his cheek. All the while he stood there with his arms folded, staring at me. He then waited until she had gone inside before approaching.

"Your mother is not going to approve of the match," he stated, and I released a sigh, put my hands to my knees and pushed myself up to standing so I could face him now.

"I don't care," I stated firmly.

"Then are you willing to just walk away from everything you have ever known?" he asked, and I folded my own arms across my chest this time, matching his demeanour and replied,

"You question my motives?" At this, her uncle released a sigh and said,

"It is getting late, and we have much more to discuss. I will be in town on the 10th, we will speak then," he said, now walking away, making me call back,

"And where will I meet you?" His reply was a strange one as he looked back over his shoulder and told me,

"I will find you, Adam, after all... finding people is what I do." His cryptic and ominous reply I found to be a troubling one. But it was also one I was not willing to let linger for too long, for I could still feel the remnants of Winnie's kiss against my lips. It made me wonder how long it would last, and it made me pray that the answer to that was long enough until the next time I could claim them.

I was quickly becoming addicted to her.

After that strange encounter with her uncle, I got into my carriage and made my way back to town. For Lucius was right, I had much to do and many things to get ready. Of course, during all of this, I realised that I had not only forgotten to declare my own love for her in return, but I had forgotten even to ask for her hand in marriage, for the moment she placed her lips on mine there was no other thoughts to be had, other than the utter joy to be claimed.

Of course, my good mood did not last, for Lucius was right, there was no way my mother was going to approve of the match. I had barely even had chance to mention her name, for after I told her that I was not going to marry Cousin Mary, this was when things got ugly between us.

"It's because of that girl, isn't it, that harlot!?" she snapped, making me grit my teeth and warn,

"Do not speak that way of her!"

"I knew it! You have been acting out of character ever since you met her, and she has been the cause! I never liked her or that man she was with!" she said looking off to one side, like some bitter old Crone. I could barely believe that she held the title of my mother, for I felt nothing for the woman before she even spoke of my Winnie, and now after such, I utterly loathed her!

"This is of little use, Mother, for it will get you nowhere!" I snapped back at her, making her scrunch up her wrinkled face, for no amount of money could make a person attractive. And I had to wonder if my mother ever had been, even before age had caught up with her.

"I promise you this, if you choose her, you will be cut off!"

"I do not care, I do not care for fortune, Mother, that is your precious John, one who needs it more than I, for be certain, Mother, as you are dead, and he is claimed at the title, his creditors will be after him like wolves smelling blood!" I threw back at her, and she gasped, holding a hand to her chest as if I had mortally wounded her with a blade.

"You see, you see, right there! You would have never spoken to me like this before… upon my word, I do not even recognise you, your father would be ashamed of you, calling you no longer a gentleman!" she threw at me, and I rolled my eyes caring little for her opinion.

"Even if you do not want the living that will be entitled for your name, you may walk away from it, but in doing so, you will also walk away from any financial living you yourself are capable of earning... I can guarantee you that!"

"You wouldn't?!" I hissed.

"Oh yes, I would, for who do you think employs you, and at my say he will sully your name in the dirt and enjoy doing it when he sees the filth and heartbreak you have brought upon this family!" It was at this point that I could stand no more, and without another word I turned on my heel and got out of there, before I said or did anything that I would never be able to take back.

It was now, when I was on the streets, that I looked up at the sky, closed my eyes and released a heavy weighted sigh. This was all before I heard a familiar voice,

"You look as though you could use a drink."

"Mr Septimus?" I questioned, before it was confirmed as he walked closer to me. He sighed and then told me,

"I never really gave much care for last name formalities, despite what convention dictates these days. Call me Lucius." I nodded, and in return told him,

"Then you'd better call me Adam."

"Very well, come on, Adam, I know a place," he said, motioning me over to his carriage and in truth, then as long as it was far from here, I was happy to go, for I was eager to be anywhere else.

"Where are we heading?" I asked as we were travelling towards Fleet Street.

"Like I said, I know a place," he replied, and I had to say I couldn't help but show my disappointment at knowing that we were not on the way to where Winnie was. Nor was she in the carriage as I had hoped she would be. Lucius' laughter drew me out of my melancholy.

"Pining after her so soon, are we?" he asked, and I was surprised.

"I must confess, you don't act like her guardian." At this he shrugged his shoulders and said,

"Well, I never claimed to be a good one. Here we are." He got out of the carriage and walked down a narrow alleyway to where the tavern was set back from the main street. Then we stepped up inside and I was greeted by dark wood that covered the entire space, one that was not considered big by any means. Dark panelled walls and dirty windows made it difficult to see much else as the glow from the fireplace constituted for most of the light. But then, despite this, I could tell that parts of it had been recently rebuilt, making me wonder if it hadn't been damaged in the great fire of London. A city that, according to the older generations, had vastly changed since.

Lucius procured us a seat and raised up his hand with two fingers before rolling his wrist and tapping on the table. This telling whoever was behind the bar that we wanted two drinks of sorts.

"Do you come here often?" I asked, and for an unknown reason, Lucius laughed.

"That sounds like something Winifred would be teasing me about, for it sounds more like you are trying to pick up a filly for the night," he exclaimed before adding,

"And yes, Adam, I come here often."

"I believe I'm right in making the assumption that you don't care what people think of you," I said, being blunt as I had a feeling he would appreciate it. At this, he smirked and as two tankards of ale were put down in front of us, he lifted one and drank a heavy gulp, before answering me,

"No, I really do not care and neither will you soon enough, that is if you choose to be with Winifred." My reply was instantaneous,

"I do... I love her."

"Oh, I know... as it's not like either of you have been subtle about the sentiment," was his dry witty remark. However, I cared little for it and now focused solely on what it might mean he would grant me.

"Then I have your approval?"

"You don't need my approval, that's the point," he answered, shocking me.

"I'm sorry?"

"You want to claim the woman as your own, yes?" he asked.

"Yes, of course," I told him in an astounded tone. He grinned and waved a hand up in a blasé motion that matched his words, telling me,

"Then you don't need my approval… your mind is set and so is hers, you are not taking her against her will and the girl loves you… you love her back. The only other things that complicate matters are the ones that you set against yourself." My mouth dropped open before I hissed,

"You're her guardian. Dear God, man, do you not care?" His eyes strangely flashed a moment as if changing colour when I mentioned God, but I knew it must have been nothing more than a trick of the light.

"It depends, are you a crazed, murdering rapist that once married to my niece, will hurt her and give her a life of misery?"

"Good God, man, no!" I shouted, suddenly standing

after banging my fist down on the table in my outrage. It felt as if something foreign and unnatural was consuming me from the inside out. It was like a power surging through my veins making me question what it was about this place. What was it about this man that seemed to draw it out of me?

In truth, I had no answers.

Only that I knew one thing for certain...

I liked it.

TWENTY

AFFAIRS OF THE HEART

I stood panting like a wild beast and Lucius merely had the audacity to smirk at me. Then he smoothed his features, cast a hand out and said,

"Sit down, Adam." His confident tone was of such that I knew it would be rare to find a man who would deny him, for there was just something powerful about him, making me wonder if he hadn't had some history of being a commander in the Navy.

I release a sigh and rubbed the bottom part of my face with my hand.

"I asked none of this to vex you, in all honesty, I like

you. You're a good sort of fellow, which is why, Adam, you should not think that I would deny the request. I have no reason to prevent such a union, nor would I want to. As far as I'm concerned, you're perfect for each other." On hearing this I could not hold on to my anger for he had given me a great compliment.

"Thank you."

"You're welcome," he said straight after drinking, his voice strained after swallowing.

"I swear they are starting to water down this ale with piss," he commented, making me spit back up into my tankard before looking down at it with disgust.

"I jest, Adam, besides, it is far safer drinking the ale than the water these days." Well, he wasn't wrong about that.

"I think the time has come for us to discuss my financial situation, for I will be honest with you, my hope was to be able to continue on at the law firm where I am based, but I fear my mother's interference will make that impossible," I told him, not relishing the turn in which this conversation had taken, but yet knowing it was one that would have to take place. For her uncle had been forthcoming with me and now I felt as if I owed it to him to do the same.

"She sounds like a delight," Lucius commented dryly, drinking some more and surprising me when he slammed it down, as it was now empty. I scoffed a laugh at his comment as he raised his hand up telling them to give us two more. I grimaced and looked down to see that I had barely touched mine and decided I'd better start drinking quicker. He nodded to me when he saw this and said,

"Good man."

"So anyway, as I was saying, I may have to take Winnie further afield and we may have to settle somewhere where they do not know my family name in hopes that my credentials are not soiled enough that I am unable to get work. This is so we can make a steady income but have no fear, for I will provide…" it was at this point he held up a hand and said,

"Let me stop you there, this is not a problem, Adam."

"It isn't?" I enquired. To which he smirked and said,

"No, it is not." Seeing as he didn't follow this up with the reasons why, I asked,

"What do you mean?"

"I'm rich, Adam, extremely so and I have no family to bestow it on," he told me, but this wasn't in a boastful manner, quite the opposite, as it was more as if he was merely stating facts.

"Lucius, you are young, no older than me I suspect… do you believe you will never marry?" At this he raised a brow at me, and our conversation stopped momentarily as our new drinks were placed on the table.

"Just trust me on this, when I say I'm not the marrying kind. In truth, Pipper is all I have."

"Pipper?" I asked not hearing the name before.

"Ah, but you do not know, her middle name is Pipper, hence why I call her such, and she has made it well known that Winnie belongs to you." At this I couldn't contain my grin.

"She said that?" I asked, making Lucius give me a knowing look himself. He didn't answer but instead went back to his drink.

"When it was decided that I was to become Pipper's ward, there were a number of reasons why I agreed to it, for the family connection is barely there, trust me on that… therefore, this was never my responsibility."

"It was one you chose?" I asked, surprised and yet not.

"You have met her, Adam, you think I would have been able to deny her anything? What I'm trying to say is that over time I have come to care for her, and it has not been simply out of duty."

"Explain… care for her?" I said in a tense tone, feeling the bitter monster of jealously lurking. He smirked and told me,

"It was a duty I thought to have been burdened with until she was married and in honesty, I never really expected to take it further, believing we would simply part ways. However, she has grown to be like a sister to me and therefore, someone that I will no doubt be keeping close to. Which is why talk of you moving away is not going to happen," he said, making me relax back against my chair, happy now at least he did not feel for her in a way that would give cause for concern or my sudden murderous jealousy. Something I confess never to feeling before meeting her, but then again this wasn't surprising considering I had never wanted anything in my entire life as much as I wanted her. Which meant these feelings were warranted and until I claimed her, I could imagine the irrational emotion was going to rear its ugly head a few times again. That was at least until our happy union could be fulfilled.

"Then what do you suppose we do, for I will not just take your money," I told him sternly.

"I admire that, but yes, Adam… *you will.*" I jerked back a little and looked at him as if he had lost his mind. Then I started to shake my head when he held up his hand and clarified,

"One day, I will explain fully to you what Pipper's been through, and I'm telling you now it is not a happy story, despite how blissfully unfazed by history she may be." This physically hurt me to hear as I couldn't stand the idea of it being true. But alas he continued, and I had to confess I was not looking forward to the day I learned more of these grievous events of her life.

"Trust me then, when I say I will never see anything like that happen to her again, for she will never go hungry, nor will she ever not have a roof over her head or a bed to sleep in… you love her, so I take it we are in agreement on this," he said in a serious tone, and I was once again astounded at hearing that it would be any different for her, that she ever could have endured the things he was saying.

"Of course, I would never allow that to happen!" I exclaimed expressively.

"Good, then you will accept the entirety of that in which I am offering… being as such, this will mean a long and happy life of luxury, for her and one she deserves. And with time, I'm sure you will deserve as well," he said, and in doing so conjuring up another thousand questions I had for him. The first of which being,

"Then what are you proposing?"

"It's simple, you love her and that means, you work for me." His answer was voiced as simple as if we had been discussing the weather.

"I work for you, in what capacity?" I asked.

"All will be known in time, but for now all you need to know is that the girl has a dowry, and it is one of a substantial amount, that will get you started in life and working for me will ensure that you will keep that way of life indefinitely… now are we in an agreement?" he said, and I found myself stunned and rendered dumbstruck.

Could it be possible that this man was about to take all of my financial worries away. Because it was true, even though I knew that my Winnie would not expect such a living, as she had made it quite clear when first meeting her what love meant to her. That it didn't come attached with an amount. But that didn't mean that I didn't want to give Winnie everything. I wanted to shower her with gifts even though I knew she'd never ask for them. I wanted to keep that soft skin of hers dressed in the finest of silks and keep her soft curves even softer through the consumption of sugary confection and hot chocolate I knew she liked.

I wanted to give her the whole world and everything in it.

And now this man offered a way for this to happen without anything from my family. It was a gift, and I was not fool enough to turn such a thing down.

"I thank you, beyond words could express and yes, we are in agreement."

"Good, then let's drink to it… another!" he shouted before slamming the second empty tanker down. Clearly, I needed to drink quicker.

I could barely believe it. I would finally be free from my family. Free to be with the woman I loved, free to travel the world if I chose and if Winnie was inclined to do so. But we could make our own decisions in forming a brand-new life together. One where the Fitzwilliam name would be no more for me.

And I for one, could not wait for that day to come.

We continued to drink, and I had to confess that after this somewhat tense conversation in the beginning, I now was finding his company a pleasing one. I enjoyed spending time with him, but I believed this was because he was very similar in some regard to my Winnie. He spoke freely and cared little for if I thought him a gentleman or not. He had great insight into the world and his historical knowledge of the past was astounding.

But there was one thing that became clear and that was a certain date that would change everything. I tried to enquire more about it, but he just continued to say that I would soon see. I would soon learn was another term he used.

I would soon be told.

It was never now, and I had to wonder what he was waiting for? Perhaps it was the security of marrying his niece that he wanted. Family secrets not dared be told until I too was classed as family. I did not know. However, what I did know was that I had been drinking for an amount of time I couldn't recall and therefore was starting to slur my words.

Soon, a girl walked over towards Lucius, and most would have believed her beautiful no doubt, but for me beauty started and ended with my Winnie, so I barely glanced at the girl. One that was now running her fingers tantalisingly across Lucius' chest and tugging at the lace at his neck. It was in this moment that he set his tankard down, suddenly stood and smacked the ass of the girl telling her,

"Go then, get your sisters and be ready for me... I will be down momentarily." The girl giggled and ran off towards the staircase of the tavern. But instead of going up to the rooms above, curiously she went down towards the cellars.

"Walk with me, Adam," he said, now grabbing his jacket from the back of his chair and throwing it over his shoulder in a casual manner. I stood, staggering before saving myself and discovering that I could indeed still walk. Then I followed him down a narrow staircase, one we both had to duck to get through, only to find it was indeed the entrance that led to the cellar. One that was unsurprisingly full of barrels. However, there was another door, and one that looked to lead nowhere but perhaps to a storage room.

"I want you to listen to me, the 14th of November is when it will all change for you, and I promise you, you will not regret any decision you make if it leads towards Winifred. You will have everything you've ever wanted, my friend... trust me." I nodded at this, taking heed of his words, despite being slightly drunk. He slapped me on my back and said,

"Good man… now go and get your affairs in order and then on the 14th, tell your mother to fuck off and pack a bag. And in doing so I promise you, if you choose to walk out that door on the day when the moon is at its highest, you will never go back."

"I understand, *I think*. Where are you going now?" At this he gave me a grin and then winked, before opening the door and telling me,

"You're not ready for what's down here yet, Adam… not yet…"

"But you soon will."

STEPHANIE HUDSON

TWENTY ONE

BEGINNING OF THE END
THE GREAT COMET
14TH NOVEMBER 1680

The moment I saw it was nightfall, I took one last look at my bedchamber knowing that from this moment on, I would never be seeing it again. In truth, I knew the thought should have troubled me. But I found myself feeling elevated more than concerned for the unknown that lay ahead. It was almost as if being with Winnie was all I would ever need and together we could face anything. I also had to confess that after my conversation only days ago with her uncle, it had at the very least, lifted some financial strain on my part.

Of course, I would have hoped he would have gone into more detail as to what he would expect of me and my given employment. But then it wasn't as if he was employing someone he didn't know and without credentials. I also didn't know why today was the day or what made it any different. For all I could tell, the only difference than any other day was what could now be seen in the sky. A bright line of light that astronomers called The Great Comet, one so vivid it was even seen in the daylight. Of course, I didn't know what consequence this had on my circumstances, but it was a pretty sight to be sure.

In all honesty, I got the sense that I was entering into some secret society and first I needed to prove such by severing all ties with my family and then marrying into his own. Not that this was a problem for me, anything but, for I could not wait to marry Winifred. By the very nature of such, the moment felt like my sole purpose for living. In truth, this day felt like the first day of the rest of my life and with only one thing left to do, I found myself eager to be on with it.

Which was why I looked around my room one more time and where there should have been melancholy, there was only happiness to see the back of it to be had. Which was why I had no problems turning my heel and leaving it behind me. Along with most things I owned, something I confess as to one time I might have deemed important enough to take with me.

After this, I made my way down to where I knew I would find my mother in her evening sitting room. Hence, why I walked in without knocking, something I knew that vexed her so, for she always liked to be prepared, was her excuse. As for me, I believed it was just another form of control she was obsessed with.

"Adam, you know better!" she snapped from behind a high backed wing chair, and I actually grinned.

"Mother, I've come to say goodbye," I stated firmly.

"For that is an odd statement, you usually just leave, Adam, without caring much a consequence it makes to me, I suspect I will see you on the morrow, do not forget, for we dine with the Chamberlains." Again, I couldn't help but grin knowing of the tedious evening I would miss.

"Then I bid you enjoy the evening, for I will not be joining you there, and nor will I be joining you anywhere else for that matter," I told her, making her frown at me.

"Adam, you are not making any sense." Oh, but she

was wrong there as this felt like the cleverest thing I had ever been about to say in my life!

"Then, let me be clear for you, Mother, I've decided that I will marry Miss Ambrogetti, with or without your blessing, for nothing will stop our union." At this she cried in outrage,

"Upon my word, it will not be!"

"That's where you are wrong, for it will and has been decided, accepted and agreed by all parties that need be involved. So, you see, there is no use even arguing against it. I have already been given the only blessing I needed which was by her guardian. We are to be wed as soon as possible," I told her, barely keeping the grin from my features. She even stamped her foot on the rug and shouted,

"Foolish boy! You really are willing to give up everything for some *foreign whore!?*" It was at this point I could stand it no longer, for I would not have anyone speaking of her like that.

"Careful what you say, Mother, for you are talking about my wife!" I snapped back, in a dangerous tone she foolishly did not heed.

"She is not your wife yet, boy! And if I have anything to say about it, then such a vile union will never take place!"

Ha vile, the only vile thing was her!

"And what exactly is it that you believe is so vile about it?" I asked, wondering after it was said why I did so, for I really didn't care for her answer.

"You have been bewitched… yes, that is it… you are too blind and irresponsible to see it! You know nothing of this woman, yet she will be the ruin of you!" she snapped bitterly, and I released a sigh. I ran a hand down my face, trying for patience and wondering if there was even any point in having this conversation any longer.

"I know of her character, Mother, far better than you ever could, she's sweet and kind and considerate and above all, she makes me happy."

"And just how happy will you be when you are cast on the streets with not a penny to your name? A name, I will remind you, is one gained by birthright, and yet here you are throwing it all away for some harlot!" Again I gritted my teeth.

"I will not allow you to speak of Miss Ambrogetti in such a manner!" I snapped back because if this was to be our last ever conversation then I was going to use the opportunity wisely. Doing so to prove to my mother once and for all, that she could not get away with saying these things about another, without first understanding the loathing that I felt towards her.

"Miss Ambrogetti, what manner of name is that!? Adam, she is a foreigner for a start but there is something more." At this she rose from her chair and upon hearing this argument yet again, I sighed in exasperation.

"Oh, not this again, Mother!" I said in a tiresome tone.

"I am telling you, my child, that girl has the Devil in her!" I confess, I threw up my hands in a dramatic sign that I was done with this. I had heard this argument before and if it wasn't gypsy spells or witchcraft, it was something to do with the Devil. It was ridiculous. So ridiculous that I needed a drink, so I walked over to a decanter of wine and poured myself a hearty glass before downing it in one. My mother's face was a picture of horror, and one in that moment, I relished in. For let her see what her son really was, I thought with a hidden grin.

"This is ridiculous!" I said to myself, before refilling the glass and drinking it down again.

"Look what she is doing to you? She has already turned you to drink." I laughed once at this in a mocking way, and shouted back at her the truth,

"No, Mother, you have!" Hearing this, she recoiled

back as if I had struck her.

"I am going to marry Winifred Ambrogetti with or without your blessing," I reaffirmed again, and once more I was not surprised by her outburst.

"No, you will not! I forbid it, your alliance would be a disgrace to the Fitzwilliam name!" Hearing this was like the last flame needed for me to boil over with anger. For did she not understand yet that I cared little for such things. In fact, I hated the name and everything it stood for in my life, for my name was a cage and one that I couldn't wait to break free of!

"Then you can keep it! I am in love with her!" I shouted, casting my arms out to the sides in my declaration, feeling the weight of it being removed as parts of that cage finally started to crumble. For I looked down upon my mother as if she had been the warden of my prison this entire time. Well, enough was enough. I would be done with this.

"Pfft, love means nothing in your duty to your family. This is your heritage, Adam, and you throw it aside for this folly," she said, now trying for some remnants of calm and I did the same, asking her a question I already knew the answer to, for she had made it quite plain.

"So, my happiness in life is not in question?" She made

a bitter face as if she didn't even know what the word meant. As though she had never had a happy day in her entire life. Had she really been that miserable to be matched with my father? For I would more likely believe it to be the other way around being married to the likes of her!

"Love is just a word and we, that are of nobility, rise above the sins of the flesh." Ha, sins of the flesh! Good Lord, if that is what making love to the woman I craved to be beneath me, then I would quite happily sign myself up to it. To an eternity of damnation to spend the rest of my life happy and swimming in sin and soaking my flesh until it consumed me!

"You think love is to be classed thus as 'sins of the flesh', you say love is a sin of men, then if that be rightly so, you can condemn me with your judgement as you see fit, but you will not stop me from marrying Miss Winifred!" I told her crossing my arms over my chest, telling her with my actions that I was unmovable in my decision.

"If you think I will condone your disgrace you are mistaken, I will see you cut off, penniless and in a poorhouse before I allow my second heir to marry a Devil's whore!" As soon as she said this, I let my anger be known, furious now unlike ever before, as I threw my glass down to the floor making it shatter. I ignored my mother's shriek of horror, something that was soon lost when I roared down at her,

"You dare talk about my future wife with such disdain and contempt!" To give the old woman her due, she stood up to me, and I wondered if this meeting would end with my hands ringing around her neck, for she seemed suicidal to push me thus.

"I do, and I will! I am ashamed of you, and you cannot be at a loss as to know why! She has poisoned your mind with her evil." I turned my back on her, just to save me from committing murder.

"And with this evil, Mother, what should we do as great nobility?" I asked with contempt and ridicule in my tone, one unsurprisingly she chose to ignore. I knew this the moment she took a deep breath as if she had broken through this madness she felt had inflicted me.

"We search deep inside ourselves, and we tear that evil out." It was at this point that I could take no more. I gave her one last look as I made my way to the door, then before I could cast my lasting thoughts upon her, I stood there, staring out into the hallway and seeing this symbolic meaning as being the last steps I would take in this house.

The last steps needed to freedom.

And I couldn't fucking wait!

I turned slowly and looked at my mother, knowing it would be the last time, then I told her,

"Then tear deeper, Mother, for you will never release me of this feeling you call evil, the very same feeling I call love. You would do better to kill me first, for as long as there is breath in my body I will be with Miss Winifred!" She sucked in a horrified breath and then snapped the most heinous of wishes upon her own child.

"Death would be better for you if it would rid you of the sinful girl that infects your soul like the plague!" At this I scoffed, not in the least bit surprised by her hateful reply. No, instead I decided to leave her with one of my own.

"You're mistaken, Mother, death would only rid me of you and this name you find all life is worth living for. But death would not rid me of the love I feel for this girl, who you deem a spawn of Hell, whether it be truth or falsehood, I just simply could not care, for our love knows no bounds and that, my dear Mother, includes you! So, I say goodbye, Mother, I shall take my leave of you for the last time." At this I walked away, and I did so without a single glance back. Not even as the last sounds I heard from my mother were the screaming ramblings of an old woman, one that I hoped would die alone and miserable as she deserved.

Finally, I closed the door, ending this chapter of my life and finding my heart lifted because of it. For now, it was time to open a new door, and for that, all I needed was to…

Find my Winnie.

TWENTY TWO

TEST OF LOVE
WINIFRED

"Do you think he'll come?" I asked for the hundredth time that day, and I think Lucius' face said it all.

"You know my reply will not have changed since the last time you asked me only ten minutes ago," he said, rubbing his forehead as though he was getting a headache. Something I knew wasn't exactly possible for a vampire.

I could barely believe that the day had finally arrived, and my entire being was in knots. I felt sick to my stomach, and it had little to do with my body and all to do with my mind. My nerves were beyond frayed, they felt as if they were unravelling, and I was barely able to keep them from making me disappear altogether.

But my fear and worry and anxiety were all warranted, for there felt as if there was so much that could go wrong, and I was scared. I was scared for so many reasons. The main one being that I didn't want to lose Adam. I didn't want to lose the man I'd fallen so much in love with, that he consumed my every thought. Days ago, when I had declared my love to him and kissed him for the first time, it was as if my entire world had found its centre.

The one soul that connected to my own.

Yet, despite this, what came next was the hardest part of all. Because I couldn't choose Adam's destiny, he had to choose it for himself. The first step was the easiest, in simply walking away from his mother. Something I knew he foolishly believed that this was all it would take. This was also something that we had no choice but to encourage him to believe. Therefore, the guilt I felt was immeasurable. I felt as if I was blindsiding him, because mortal life was so precious, because living it was a danger they faced daily. Everything could kill them. Be it an accident, or an attack. War or starvation. Even the invisible enemy known as disease, could take them without even the knowledge of being infected, and because of this uncertainty, it made every moment lived through more treasured.

I knew this, for I had witnessed mortal life in all its forms many times over. Their short cycles of life that flashed me by in an instant. It was like clicking your fingers for an immortal, one moment it was there and the next it was gone.

This meant that there weren't many that would openly choose to die for love, and tonight that was precisely what I was going to have to ask him to do. And because of it...

I was terrified.

Utterly terrified for two reasons, and both of which counteracted each other, for if he said yes, I knew of all the possibilities in which it could go wrong. And if he said no, then I knew then he would be lost to me forever, because it was forbidden for a supernatural being to be with a mortal. Unless that mortal was fated to you by the Gods themselves there was no hope, and for us because he had only been fated to me with claiming the Beast in mind. And as for me, I had only been fated to him and allowed to keep him until the one night that it was made possible to merge his soul with another in Hell.

So yes, I was scared, for I knew that if this went wrong,

I wouldn't just be losing one mortal I loved, but I would also be losing the Beast down in Hell, *I had also already fallen in love with.*

"Relax, little Imp, worrying about the outcome will not change it, no matter how much you wear out my carpet with your pointless journeys upon it," Lucius said from his chair.

"Fine, then tell me the plan again," I said, coming to sit opposite him with a sigh. Our relationship since the first moment he saved me seemed to have changed daily, as I looked upon him now like a brother. He was my family, and right now he was the only one I had. He had taken care of me far more than I knew was what had been expected of him. I may have started out as an assignment ordered by his King, but I had become much more to him than that. Despite knowing he would grumble about admitting it, something I enjoyed teasing him about, and often.

He released a sigh and put down the book he was reading.

"Alright, little Imp… here it is again… just like the first day you met him, we will fake an attack. After all, there is enough wasteful flesh out there that would no doubt take advantage of a pretty girl." At this I smirked and said,

"Aww, and I am to be the pretty bait… I feel so special." He scoffed a laugh as I knew he would.

"After which, Adam will come in and save the day and you will give him his choice. For fighting a group of men to save the woman he loves would no doubt end badly for him and he would be a fool not to know it."

"And then what, if he chooses me… what then?" I asked, as this was the part I was most concerned about.

"Then, unfortunately, my dear, comes the hard part, as he will have to die and forfeit his mortal life before the Beast will accept him as a vessel." I released an even heavier sigh at this, slumping down in my chair. But then his confident face troubled me.

"What exactly are you not telling me…? Oh, don't look at me like that, I know you by now," I said, recognising the glint in his eye as it momentarily glowed crimson.

"All right, I will tell you, but try to refrain from another girlie outburst that includes screaming."

"Lucius." I said his name in warning.

"I have been instructed to turn him into a vampire." At this, I shot out of my chair and shouted,

"WHAT!"

"I believe that constitutes as a girlie outburst," he

responded dryly, after wincing as if the noise I made hurt his ears.

"I don't care! Now explain it to me... how long have you known this?" I demanded.

"Calm down, Pip, take your seat and I will explain." I did as he said and sat back down in my chair, knowing that I would get nothing from him until I had done this. He was demanding in that way.

"Without being turned into one of my kind, he will not be strong enough to survive. Abaddon will simply rip him apart, he has to be immortal and strong enough to take something as powerful as this," he said quickly, no doubt to stop me from reacting until he had finished.

"And just when were you planning to tell me?" I asked again.

"Honestly, just before it happened," he said, making my eyes bulge.

"Lucius!"

"Look, I know you are worried but trust me, Pipper... it's the only way," he said with sincerity.

"But I thought you couldn't turn a human," I said, knowing this to be true.

"There is but one way for me to turn a human, but in

this case, that will not be needed." I frowned, as this wasn't exactly what I would have classed as an answer. But as I was about to open my mouth to point this out, he held up a hand to stop me.

"Adam is fated to become one of mine."

"And how do you know this, how can you be so sure?" I enquired now he would let me speak again.

"Because Adam isn't just fated to you, he's also fated to me." Hearing this I gasped, then asked in whispered tones,

"What do you mean?"

"There was a reason I was appointed this task, one that was set by the Oracle herself, despite the order being voiced from the King. Adam, is fated to become a vampire and the two of you will then forever be entwined in my life."

"Well, I guess that's good, considering I like you." At this he smirked and said,

"The feeling is mutual, my dear."

"So, it really is all fate." This is when he went on to tell me what I knew to be true.

"Everything is prophesied, little Imp, and one day I believe that you and Adam will play your own part in something far greater… but until then, we're standing at the very beginning of that fated path. In truth, what lies ahead is an unknown, but unless we take the first steps, then the destination will never be ours." I thought on this and couldn't help but then ask,

"And what of your intentions for Adam and his beast?"

"What of them?" he asked taken aback.

"Do you… wish to use him?" At this he frowned at me and answered with a stern, and resounding,

"No." I wanted to believe him as he had not given me cause not to, but I had to be sure.

"I don't want to offend you, but you must understand my reasons for asking such, for he will be loyal to you."

"So, and what of it?" he asked, as if he really didn't understand my meaning.

"So, what is to stop you using him just like Lucifer would?" At this I saw him tense his jaw, as if he was grinding his teeth and trying to calm his anger. Then he leaned forward and told me in a very serious tone,

"Because Abaddon is not the only creature the Devil created for his own gain." The way he said this shocked me and I sucked in a startled breath as the implication was clear,

"You?" I hissed out the question, asking myself how I could have missed something like this. But then again, Lucius hadn't exactly been forthcoming this last month in regard to his history.

"The Devil is my father," he stated suddenly, and I gasped.

"You're the Devil's son! But... but you told me you were born human?" I said, throwing back his own words at him and trying to make sense of them, hoping he would help me.

"I was born human but let us just say that Lucifer had a different idea."

"Alright, Lucius, you are going to have to explain this to me here," I said, rubbing my forehead and seeing the way he looked at me now I was not surprised, as the Lucius I had come to learn, was not a man that responded well to having demands made of him. But then I also came to quickly understand that he treated me far differently than he had ever treated anyone else. To begin with, his patience never seemed to run out, although I could see it was probably coming close to it now as he leaned forward and told me,

"My life and how it began is not common knowledge

for a reason, Imp, so what I say now goes no further than this room, understood?" I nodded, scooting into the end of my seat waiting to hear the rest of his story.

"I was created by Lucifer once my life as a human was no more. So, you see, the Beast you love is not the only beast that was made. I know what it is like to be created as a tool for power. Lucifer needed someone to control the vampire race, so he made me. But make no mistake, I am not his puppet and nor would I ever make Abaddon mine." He said this in such a way that I could not deny it being anything other than truth. One he continued to keep telling me.

"So, trust me, if there was anyone in this world you would choose to become Adam's maker, it would be the only person that has no ambition to takeover Hell and kill Lucifer." I released a sigh the moment he finished, knowing now that I could have faith in his words, telling him,

"Alright… so you make a good point."

"As I usually do, little Imp… as I usually do." He repeated an aside before reaching for his glass and swigging back the rest of his drink. Then, looking at the clock, he told me,

"It is time."

"Time for what exactly, that's the question?" I said, wishing that someone knew the outcome. Lucius offered me his hand and helped me rise from my seat and once standing opposite him, he tipped my face back with a hold on my chin and then he told me,

"It is time for the beginning of the end for Adam Fitzwilliam." I nodded, accepting this for there was no other way. Because I had argued with myself and struggled with my moral compass, asking which way it pointed to. To be sure I wanted Adam like no other and having him combined with Abaddon... well, that would have been granting me everything I had ever wanted. Everything all wrapped up into one being I could love more than anything else in the world. But then I also knew that love was a sacrifice, and just as he was potentially willing to sacrifice his own life to be with me, I was willing to sacrifice being with him to save his life.

I had been willing to walk away, hoping that he may meet some kind woman who would treat him right and he could potentially live out the rest of his days not knowing the truth. But then Lucius had explained to me, that Adam could have quite easily been hit by that carriage that very day. He would have died without ever knowing what it felt like to be truly in love.

To be given the choice to sacrifice himself to an unknown fate because it was the right thing to do was something I knew deep down Adam would accept.

Because sometimes sacrifice is all the choice we have, and tonight…

Adam would have to make that choice one more time.

A sacrifice for love.

TWENTY THREE

A LOVING SACRIFICE

ADAM

I don't know how it happened, but I found myself in what was known as the Pool of London. It was a stretch of the River Thames from London Bridge to below Limehouse. Part of the Tideway of the Thames, the Pool was navigable by tall-masted vessels bringing into the city coastal and overseas goods. The Pool of London was divided into two parts, the Upper Pool and Lower Pool, with places in between that were low-income houses or what was known as slums.

I had to confess I was surprised when Lucius got word

to me of this being the place I was to come to. That this was where I would find Winifred. In fact, as soon as a messenger came up to me in the street, being just a young boy, and handed me the note, I had become wary. A single address on a piece of paper and a line telling me where I would find her, was signed off by Lucius himself. From here on out, it therefore had me questioning everything happening from that moment on. But this was secondary to the panic I felt, for I knew that Winifred should not be in this particular area of London, for it was not safe. Hence, me getting here quickly, and now making my way towards the back of the tavern where the piece of paper stated she would be.

The smell was always worse around these parts, for people cared little about simply throwing their own excrement outside the window and onto the streets they themselves would travel. In truth, the people here were barely living, as it was a cutthroat world for them existing day to day, and not knowing how long they had left, or where their next meal would come from for that matter. It was life at its most basic form and one purely of survival, as being without a job or a means to feed yourself or your family, basically meant you were living on borrowed time.

I could not imagine a life like this, and I only found myself glad that my future with Winnie did not look this bleak. Especially not now with the offer that Lucius had bestowed upon me. I did not need all the riches in the world, all I asked for was enough to make Winnie happy and to be living in comfort. Of course, I would have loved nothing more than to lavish her with everything she had ever desired. But looking at this place now and I knew I would have been content with a roof over our heads. Some simple and nice furnishings that made our life comfortable, and a continued wage that would mean we would never have to worry about putting food on the table.

In short, life would have been content and the two of us together, living within our means, would have been a home full of happiness and laughter. Which made me wonder now what Winnie could be doing in such a place, such Hell on Earth was no place for my Winnie.

A man passed me by, staggering down the street and barely stopping long enough to vomit on himself before staggering off again on his way. I wrinkled my nose in disgust, wishing to be done with it, *whatever this was to be*. Another building over offered the sight of two men fucking a woman like animals, and had she not had her head thrown back in ecstasy, I would have been worried she was being taken against her will.

But I was not naive enough not to realise that things like this happened in the world. I just admit to turning a blind eye to most of it, for there was little to be done by just one man such as I.

It had to be said the docks were busy even at night, and I had to question the type of clientele a tavern around these parts would serve. At least the air was fresher here and didn't smell so badly of excrement. The inn was on the corner of a street that I didn't know the name of, and it had already cost me a coin to have this direction so far. But it was here, upon walking up that I heard her voice, and the moment I did, it filled me with pure horror, for it was not her usual voice of excitement but one of…

Fear.

"No! Get off me! Help!" This was when I started to run towards the back of the inn and into an alleyway that ran behind it.

"Winifred!?" I shouted her name as I ran as fast as I could. Once there I took in the scene very quickly, and what met me was the core of all my nightmares! For there was my Winnie being attacked by three brutes, that all seemed to want a piece of her!

"Adam…? Oh, Adam, please help me!" Winnie cried out to me as she struggled with the three men, and without hesitation I ran to her aid, now knowing that I did so with the possible outcome of my death. But I would have laid my life down for her willingly, just to save her own!

But then in that moment something had overtaken me and consumed me completely. A blinding rage unlike any other I had ever experienced, as I threw myself into the man closest to me, tackling him to the ground. I threw my fists around, connecting with whatever flesh I could and in my rage, I knew that I was receiving just as many blows. Yet I did not feel the pain of it. No, I was too lost in my fury to feel anything but the anger coursing through my veins.

Unfortunately, it was not enough as I felt my body being picked up by two of them behind me. I felt myself sag between the pillars of muscle that stood either side and the biggest one that I had been punching, turned swiftly and punched me in the gut. This was a second before the two men dropped me so that I fell to the floor. My palms saved me from falling completely, yet it was not enough to prevent the blood from spewing out of my lips. I knew then that I was badly hurt, but still, I would not give in.

I heard the bastards laughing at me as I was picked up again and slammed against the wall.

"So ye thinks of spoiling me bit of fun do ye, by taking me whore for thyself?" I let these words sink in and fuel my rage, calling it back as I lifted my head and stared at him. In that moment I knew, had I been fortunate enough to have a blade in my hand, I would have run him through. Doing so without a moment's hesitation. I wanted this man to die. I wanted to feel his flesh split beneath my hands and his bones break beneath my feet. I knew I should have been concerned by these murderous thoughts that were running rampant through my mind, but as of yet... strangely, *they felt right.*

It was in this moment I made the decision that if I was to die then I would do so trying to save the woman I loved, for nothing else mattered! So, I spat blood out in his face and yanked one of the men that was holding me at the side into the oncoming assault from my head. This ended with me cracking my forehead against his nose and making it burst. The man who had been holding most of my weight now fell unsteadily and all three of us fell to the floor. It was in this moment I took advantage, quickly pounding my fists into one of the men that still had hold of me. Then, when he seemed subdued enough from the continuous blows of my fists, I took a moment to breathe. However, the second he tried to crawl away I grabbed him by his hair and smashed his face into the ground.

After this he stopped moving so I got to my feet, now facing the biggest of all three. I was shaking in my rage but at the very least I was not foolish enough not to see the threat as he pulled out a dirty blade. However, the moment he turned this on my Winnie was when my blood ran cold, freezing in my veins. He held it at her throat, and I watched as tears now ran down her sweet face, making your eyes look like emeralds sparkling in the night.

"Let my woman go!" I said with deadly calm, barely recognising my own voice. Once more I knew that I had sustained some injuries and was bleeding from many places on my body... I potentially had been stabbed at some point during the scuffle, but like before, I felt no pain and knew the only agony that I would endure was if that blade managed to break the skin of the woman I loved.

Speaking of the woman I loved, as those tears continued to fall, she used the last of her strength to speak to me.

"Adam, don't... just go while you still can," she

implored, the tears now coming quicker. I started to shake my head and told her in a soft voice,

"I'm afraid I can't do that, my love."

"Adam, please, I want you to live, my life isn't worth you dying over… you don't know who I am." This last part was said as barely a whisper, and my mother's words started to ring in my ears. All of the unnatural things she had accused her of being suddenly hammered home in my mind. I wondered if such a thing was possible and, in that moment, I knew the truth. That even if it was, I couldn't care less. I didn't care what she was, I only cared for who she was to me. *And that was enough.* That was enough to risk my life for the woman I loved, despite the outcome of learning the truth. For no truth would ever prevent me from loving her!

"I don't care if you were born in the fires of Hell and were made of the damned souls down there, I LOVE YOU!" I shouted, and to a point that even the man behind her flinched. It was if he could sense that I was out of my mind and even if he killed her, he too would then die. For if he took her from me, I would have nothing to live for.

"But you will die!" Winifred answered in a heart-breaking tone that told me she did not want this for me.

She did not want me to sacrifice my life for her own. But it did not matter, for she said this now because she loved me. She loved me just as I loved her... and that sacrifice now went both ways.

Which is why I told her,

"Yes... but today I die a man, a man saving the woman he loves, today... *I die for you.*" This last part felt like a goodbye, and therefore was pushed through the emotions that were trying to make it stick in my throat. I looked down for only a moment to see the blood draining from my body and pooling at my feet, knowing that I possibly did not have long, for there was too much blood. But then the moment I looked up was when I made my move.

A move, that in the end... *I didn't need to make.*

As this was when I saw the true side of Winnie, as something in her snapped. Like a veil had been lifted and what I saw underneath was even more astounding than what I already believed her to be.

"Good, it's about bloody time!" she said, actually smiling, and then quicker than my eyes could track, she had her assailant in her grasp and simply snapped his neck. Twisting it as if he had been made of nothing more than dry kindling. She let his body go, making it fall to the ground in a heap of dead flesh and bone. Then, as if she had not just murdered a man, she smoothed her hands down her dress and straightened her little hat before stepping over his body, as if it had been no more than a bag of flour stood in her way.

I was rendered mute and unmoving, for I could do little but stare at her in astonishment. Then after she came over to me, it was only when her voice asked a question that I tore my eyes away from the destruction she had caused. A death delivered so easily that it should have frightened me.

But it didn't.

"You love me?" she asked sweetly, and I felt her hand touch my face, forcing my gaze back to hers, where she asked me again,

"You love me?"

"Yes!" I said, all but shouting this, for I didn't care what she had done or how she had managed it. Especially for someone with such a slight of frame as she. But this was when she asked me,

"You trust me?" I nodded my head, telling her silently that I did and wondering now what part of this was relevant.

A deadly answer to which...

I was soon to find out.

TWENTY FOUR

BORN AGAIN

Winnie cupped my cheek before pushing my hair back from my face, doing so even though I knew I was now bloody. She had asked me if I trusted her, and I did with my life. One that in this moment I felt was now leaving me, doing so with every second I took breath. I knew this was the end, for I could feel it coming closer. But still I uttered a single answer without taking my eyes from hers.

"Yes."

I did trust her, and if there was one last sight I wanted to lay witness to before I took my last breath, it would be her beautiful face. Those eyes that I had fallen in love with the first moment I had seen them staring back up at me. The look of love she gave me right now was an everlasting gift. One that I hoped I was able to hold onto into the next life. She was so sweet, despite what I had seen her do moments ago, as she carefully wiped the blood away from my lips before kissing me.

I used the last of my strength to return the passion that she so willingly bestowed upon me. I cared little for the death that lay around us in that moment, for I could only feel the true depth of love in what I knew would most likely be our last kiss. The moment she could feel me losing strength was when she cupped my face with both hands. She angled it towards her shorter height, then she asked me the oddest question.

"And do you love me enough to die for me?" I took in a weighted breath, trying to make sense of what it was she asked of me. Surely, she should know by now. For the fact was about to come true and become a proven conclusion to our time together. It felt as if everything had stopped around us. As if God himself had created this moment just for the two of us, and if this was to be my goodbye, then I wanted her to know the truth from my own lips, for

I feared now that my actions were not enough. So, after looking up into the night sky and seeing it as I had that night I spent time with her. The differences of such may have been many but with the great comet now travelling through the vast darkness, I knew the time was right. So, I told her,

"Yes, I would die for you." As soon as I said this, death quickly descended and not in the form that I had believed it to be, for I had gathered that I would simply fall to my knees and fade away until my last breath was heard giving way to death. However, this did not happen, as I was suddenly grabbed from behind, believing it to be one of my assailants that had come back for revenge. However, a tight hold on my hair was used to yank my head to one side, exposing my neck. Then, before I could even utter a distressed sound, I felt pain. Immense pain of the likes that burst beneath my flesh as it felt as if I were being ripped open at the neck. It took me a moment to realise, but lips were attached to fangs that had been plunged into my flesh.

My widened frightened eyes went to my Winifred, my love, as I saw great tears fall down her cheeks. This was when she looked up at the sky, seeing the comet as I had done. I saw now that she had something clasped in her hand. They looked like small stones that I could barely see between her fist. She lifted them to her heart and said,

"The time is now, Abaddon, the time is now to take your place in the world and be with us… to be with me." A light above me started to shine brighter and I wondered if this was it, was it the comet that would claim us all? I didn't know, only that it felt as if something greater than us all was being summoned here.

It made me question if my Winnie was a witch of some kind, and this was her casting a spell. I watched as she closed her eyes and shuddered as if she felt something that none of us could see. As for me, I was fading fast as that light was growing brighter and brighter all around me.

"Now, Lucius!" I heard Winnie shout before I felt the pressure of her hand held flat to my chest, with the stones caught in between. The effect of this felt like I had been struck by lightning, as my heart was pounding hard enough I felt as though it would burst through my ribs, straight out of my flesh and into the awaiting hands of the woman I loved. After this, I felt the slight pressure that had once been at my neck leave me and arms belonging to someone else were now holding me up. I felt my head fall forward as if it near impossible to hold it any other way, for I had no strength left in me.

I heard voices but I could not distinguish what they were saying. I wondered briefly whether they were trying to give me aid, for I felt pressure pressed against the wound at my side and the cause of my great blood loss. I vaguely thought that this didn't make any sense, for why would they be trying to save me, after being the ones that tried to kill me first? But then I felt something wet being placed against my lips. I tried to turn my face away from it, but this was in vain.

"Drink child, and become one of us, drink for the woman you love." I heard a voice I recognised speak softly behind me and it took me a moment to realise who it belonged to.

Lucius

I don't know why, but something compelled me to do as I was asked, as if I could deny this man nothing, so I started to drink. Now taking in great gulps of the liquid that was held out in front of me that had me suckling shamefully like a babe, and then when enough of it was consumed, I knew this was it. I felt myself leaving my body for the last time, and I opened my mouth as the last breath finally left me.

"Adam... Adam... don't go far, don't go too far." In the vast darkness I could hear her voice, yet it was strange, for I felt as if I had no body. As if I had no ears to hear and no eyes to see. I felt nothing. But that voice that surrounded me became such a comfort to me that I wanted to do anything it asked. Then suddenly I started to feel once more. I felt myself being pulled one way and I knew it was the opposite to what she wanted so I stayed. I don't know how but I merely had to think of what I wanted, and the feeling of motion stopped. The feeling as if my mind was being dragged one way ceased to exist and because of it, I heard her voice again,

"That's good... that's good, Adam. Stay with me, promise you'll stay with me and not leave for I have someone I wish for you to meet." Had I the ability other than thought, I would have asked her who, but it was as if she could read my mind.

"His name is Abaddon, and you are destined to become one. It is fated. Now all you have to do is let him in and then we can all be together. Open your heart out to him, Adam, welcome him into your body and I will be here waiting for you on the other side once you do. Please, Adam, I need you... I love you."

The moment I heard this I suddenly came back to myself as if I was being catapulted back into my body. And as I did so, I found my first action to be screaming in the night. I cried out in utter agony as every movement felt like torture. I thrashed around trying everything I could to escape it, but it was useless. I felt the weight of being held down at the shoulders, and someone sat on the front of my body as if trying to keep me steady and locked to the ground. Then, when I heard her voice, I knew who it was above me.

"That's it, you've found me, you found me at last," she said just as I felt as if my body was about to be ripped apart from the inside out. My screams of suffering however were left unaccounted for, and all I was left to do was shake and tremble in hopes of trying to stop the agonising pain. One that had overtaken every inch of my body. I felt as if every bone was being broken and my muscles were growing to the point that they would split my skin. I was literally being ripped apart, and for some strange reason, it wasn't killing me.

"No, listen to me, Abaddon, this is your new host, take him, take care of him and we can be together. NO! Take care of him!" Winifred shouted in clear panic this time, and I could feel her lips against my forehead as she tried to hold my head steady. It was as if she was communicating with the very being that was trying to tear me apart. As if she was trying to get him to accept me instead of fight against me. I didn't know if she would ever succeed, for I screamed again as another round of pain tore through me.

"LISTEN TO ME!" she was screaming now, sobbing out her own panic, crying out to him, this unknown beast I could now feel growling and snarling at me. It was him that she was talking to now, not me. She was trying to get him to accept me, and I knew that she needed help.

"I love you both and now you are to become one, take care of my love for me and you will get my love in return," she said this more softly this time, and her voice had an instant effect, for he calmed enough so he could now listen to my own voice of reason. It was strange, as I knew that what I said now would not be heard by anyone else, for the words would not be formed by my lips but instead in my mind.

'Hear what she says, Beast, for if you love her as I do, you will do as she says. Do not fight. Do not fight as I know you want to. I can feel you there. *I can feel your rage,* but if you love her, you will let it go, and claim what

I offer you now. If you love her as I, then we will live as one. As one entity, so we both may share her… share her for an eternity together and in doing so, nothing will be strong enough to ever take her away from us again… I promise you.' After I said this the pain suddenly stopped, and the rumbling sound of a beast was all I heard, knowing now that this was his acceptance.

Then… *came silence.*

I questioned how I knew any of these things, wondering if it hadn't been Winifred herself that had somehow given me this knowledge. Either way it all became clear, the one she had once spoken about being the most painful to lose was the Beast she had grown to love.

I was suddenly hit with eighty years of their life together in Hell. I saw it all in in a flash of moments when I connected with him. *He loved her.* He loved her more than anything else in the world and she had quickly become his reason for living. Before then all he had ever known was rage and a burning desire to destroy.

Until there was her.

And they had taken her from him! And since that moment he had vowed to do anything to get her back, and his only option to do so, *had been me.* I felt the injustice of this on his behalf, already feeling protective of him. It was strange because whereas before I would have felt a jealous rage, now I did not. For now, I had two people to protect in life, one being Winnie and the other now being my Beast.

And he in turn felt the same about me. For as soon as he accepted me, it was the first time he felt at peace since he'd had his Winifred. That was the moment we became one and everything suddenly felt right. As if my fate had just slotted into a place that had now been cemented there, carving out a future, an eternity where Winifred and I could be together forever.

"Wake up to your new life, my love, wake up to your new birth." I heard my little Winnie say, with her lips against my forehead before they moved down and were placed against my lips. The feel of them against my own was when I breathed in for the first time, taking in her essence. Then I was assaulted with discovery, as there was now a whole new depth of the world around me. I sat up quickly, and felt a body slumped next to me. But then when I felt that my girl was about to fall due to my abrupt movements, I quickly grabbed her.

I was amazed at the speed of my body.

It was incredible.

I then cast my gaze to the side to see it was Lucius who I had knocked to the ground. For the moment I ignored this, and pulled Winnie closer to me, now taking more care to do so, so as not to crush her. For strangely, I now knew that I could. I knew it because of the strength I now felt coursing through my body. It was as though I could feel every inch of me coming alive for the first time. What she said was true…

I felt reborn.

Reborn into something faster, stronger and more powerful than the once mere human man that I had been.

I didn't know what I was, but two things were certain, one was the Beast I could feel content inside me, and the second was the overwhelming urge I had to hold Winnie to me and keep her there forever. To make love to her, to treasure her, and to protect her. Which is why the first words out of my mouth that I said to her, were the very same that were spoken when first seeing her.

"Turtle Dove?" I asked, questioning if this was real, for the voice I heard was not one of my own. It was deeper. Stronger.

"Yes, Adam, I am here… I will always be here," she replied through a veil of emotion that was making it difficult to form the words for her.

"I feel... different... stronger, by the Gods I feel strong! I feel... like something is there... something great is waiting inside of me," I said, telling her how I felt, doing so with astonishment in my tone. She cupped my cheek and told me,

"I know... I know you do but you have to control it. You are the Beast now, you have both become one with each other and it is under your command... you have to listen to me, Adam... you have to be strong enough to contain it, he is keeping you safe, but you have to do the same for him." I nodded, letting it be known that I understood.

"I know... I can feel him there. He's... he's talking to me, can you hear him?" At my question, she looked up to the sky as if listening for something and this time when a tear fell from beneath a line of thick lashes, it was not one created by grief or pain or fear...

It was happiness.

I knew that when she said,

"No, I can't hear him anymore, but you can and now you must command him to stay there until you are ready."

"Ready for what?" I asked, making her look away as if ashamed by what she had done to me. I couldn't stand to see her pain, so I grasped her chin and forced her to look back at me, trying to remain gentle in my actions.

"Winifred, you must tell me," I commanded her softly, telling her that I wasn't angry, that I just needed to know.

"Ready for the Beast to arise," she muttered as tears fell down her cheeks and I caught them with my thumbs, wiping them away before banishing her worries. Letting her know that she would not be faced with my anger and telling her,

"Then we have much to do to ready ourselves, for I find myself looking forward to the day." Hearing this, my Winnie looked back at me and this time her eyes started to glow, as if the true essence of her being was shining back at me. I was overcome by such a sight, I found my instincts taking over, and where as a mere human I would not have once been so bold, now something else in me snapped. It was simple, and raw and primal.

It was the need to claim.

So, I grabbed her by the back of the neck, and pulled her hard against me, kissing her now in a way that I had never done before. I didn't just let her lead and softly taste her lips, as if fearful it would be too much for her. No, now it felt as though I was trying to brand myself to her, claiming the kiss and dominating every aspect of it. Making her mine and in doing so, ensuring she knew who owned her!

And she fucking loved it!

She relished every second of it that I gave her. I could feel it down to my core, she wanted me to master her, and in doing so, I in turn would become her slave. I knew I would do anything for this woman, and right now the need to be inside her, was almost too great to bear. I felt myself getting lost in the kiss, one deep enough that it felt as if I was connecting with her soul… as if we both were…

Beast and I.

We were one, and we both wanted to claim her!

Something I would have no doubt done, had not the sound of someone clearing his throat penetrated the air and brought me back to my senses. For I knew there was no way I could first claim the woman I loved here in the dirty slums of London. The thought of it actually made me laugh, knowing how easily I could have lost my head to my beautiful Winnie.

So, I stood, doing so easily, and picking her up as if she weighed nothing at all. God, I was strong. I felt exhilarated, as if nothing could best me. But when I looked back to

Lucius was when I felt something even greater inside me. A sense of knowing. An understanding that didn't need words said to me. Just as I had done when first encountering the Beast that was trying to combine with me. Which was why I quickly stated what I felt in my heart and my very being.

"You are my father!" Lucius smirked and nodded his head once, and suddenly it all made sense. Everything he had said to me when drinking in the tavern about me one day being ready. This was what he meant. It had been their plan all along. I knew I should have been angry. I knew I should have felt a bitter betrayal from those that I had trusted, but strangely I didn't. Strangely, I just felt that they had been the ones to lead me to this destiny, one that was always mine to claim.

And besides, in doing so meant that I got my wish. I was free, and in a way that I never thought possible. Free to live however I wanted and to do so with the woman I loved by my side. Which was why I made my next claim, doing so with the strength of my words being known in my tone.

"Then you will lay witness to our marriage and make my world complete. I want this day to mark the beginning in all ways." At this, my little Winnie jumped up excitedly and I caught her in my arms. Then, as I looked down at her, I finally got to ask the question I had wanted to upon first laying eyes on her.

"Say you will be my wife, Winifred, say it now." At this she cupped my cheek and told me,

"Nothing would give me more pleasure, or more happiness in this world than being yours... I love you, Adam."

"I love you too, Winnie... we both do," I told her, now walking with her cradled in my arms and with my maker by my side. For I knew that not only was I now a vampire, a child of the King that stood next to me. But I was something so much more...

I was the most powerful being ever created.

The Devil's only fear.

I was Adam. I was Abaddon.

and I was...

A Beast that belonged to an Imp.

The End of Book 2

To be continued

In…

Shadow Imp Series

Book 3

ACKNOWLEDGEMENTS

Well first and foremost my love goes out to all the people who deserve the most thanks and are the wonderful people that keep me going day to day. But most importantly they are the ones that allow me to continue living out my dreams and keep writing my stories for the world to hopefully enjoy... These people are of course YOU! Words will never be able to express the full amount of love I have for you guys. Your support is never ending. Your trust in me and the story is never failing. But more than that, your love for me and all who you consider your 'Afterlife family' is to be commended, treasured and admired. Thank you just doesn't seem enough, so one day I hope to meet you all and buy you all a drink! ;)

To my family... To my amazing mother, who has believed in me from the very beginning and doesn't believe that something great should be hidden from the world. I would like to thank you for all the hard work you put into my books and the endless hours spent caring about my words and making sure it is the best it can be for everyone to enjoy. You make Afterlife shine. To my wonderful crazy father who is and always has been my hero in life. Your strength astonishes me, even to this day and the love and care you hold for your family is a gift you give to the Hudson name. And last but not least, to the man that I consider my soul mate. The man who taught me about real love and makes me not only want to be a better person but makes me feel I am too. The amount of support you have given me since we met has been incredible and the greatest feeling was finding out you wanted to spend the rest of your life with me when you asked me to marry you.

All my love to my dear husband and my own personal Draven... Mr Blake Hudson.

Another personal thank you goes to my dear friend Caroline Fairbairn and her wonderful family that have embraced my brand of crazy into their lives and given it a hug when most needed.

For their friendship I will forever be eternally grateful.

I would also like to mention Claire Boyle my wonderful PA, who without a doubt, keeps me sane and constantly smiling through all the chaos which is my life ;) And a loving mention goes to Lisa Jane for always giving me a giggle and scaring me to death with all her count down pictures lol ;)

Thank you for all your hard work and devotion to the saga and myself. And always going that extra mile, pushing Afterlife into the spotlight you think it deserves. Basically helping me achieve my secret goal of world domination one day…evil laugh time… Mwahaha! Joking of course ;)

As before, a big shout has to go to all my wonderful fans who make it their mission to spread the Afterlife word and always go the extra mile. I love you all x

ABOUT THE AUTHOR

Stephanie Hudson has dreamed of being a writer ever since her obsession with reading books at an early age. What first became a quest to overcome the boundaries set against her in the form of dyslexia has turned into a life's dream. She first started writing in the form of poetry and soon found a taste for horror and romance. Afterlife is her first book in the series of twelve, with the story of Keira and Draven becoming ever more complicated in a world that sets them miles apart.

When not writing, Stephanie enjoys spending time with her loving family and friends, chatting for hours with her biggest fan, her sister Cathy who is utterly obsessed with one gorgeous Dominic Draven. And of course, spending as much time with her supportive partner and personal muse, Blake who is there for her no matter what.

Author's words.

My love and devotion is to all my wonderful fans that keep me going into the wee hours of the night but foremost to my wonderful daughter Ava...who yes, is named after a cool, kick-ass, Demonic bird and my sons, Jack, who is a little hero and Baby Halen, who yes, keeps me up at night but it's okay because he is named after a Guitar legend!

Keep updated with all new release news & more on my website www.afterlifesaga.com

Never miss out, sign up to the mailing list at the website.

Also, please feel free to join myself and other Dravenites on my Facebook group Afterlife Saga Official Fan

Interact with me and other fans. Can't wait to see you there!

ALSO BY
STEPHANIE HUDSON

Afterlife Saga

Afterlife

The Two Kings

The Triple Goddess

The Quarter Moon

The Pentagram Child /Part 1

The Pentagram Child /Part 2

The Cult of the Hexad

Sacrifice of the Septimus /Part 1

Sacrifice of the Septimus /Part 2

Blood of the Infinity War

Happy Ever Afterlife /Part 1

Happy Ever Afterlife / Part 2

The Forbidden Chapters

*

Transfusion Saga

Transfusion

Venom of God

Blood of Kings
Rise of Ashes
Map of Sorrows
Tree of Souls
Kingdoms of Hell
Eyes of Crimson
Roots of Rage
Heart of Darkness
Wraith of Fire
Queen of Sins

*

King of Kings
Dravens Afterlife
Dravens Electus

*

Kings of Afterlife
Vincent's Immortal Curse
The Hellbeast King

*

The Shadow Imp Series
Imp and the Beast
Beast and the Imp

*

Afterlife Academy: (Young Adult Series)

The Glass Dagger

The Hells Ring

*

Stephanie Hudson and Blake Hudson

The Devil in Me

OTHER AUTHORS AT HUDSON INDIE INK

Paranormal Romance/Urban Fantasy

Sloane Murphy

Xen Randell

C. L. Monaghan

Sorcha Dawn

Sci-fi/Fantasy

Devin Hanson

Crime/Action

Blake Hudson

Mike Gomes

Contemporary Romance

Gemma Weir

Elodie Colt

Ann B. Harrison

Lightning Source UK Ltd.
Milton Keynes UK
UKHW010627160622
404514UK00003B/26

9 781913 904975